7/13

HE

Also by Sara Pritchard

Crackpots

Lately

HELP WANTED: FEMALE

Stories

Sara Pritchard

etruscan press

Etruscan Press
Wilkes University
84 West South Street
Wilkes-Barre, PA 18766
(570) 408-4546

WILKES UNIVERSITY

www.etruscanpress.org

Published 2013 by Etruscan Press
Printed in the United States of America
Design by Julianne Popovec
The text of this book is set in Goudy Old Style

First Edition

13 14 15 16 17 5 4 3 2 1

Library of Congress Cataloging-in-Publication Data

Pritchard, Sara.
  Help wanted: female : stories / Sara Pritchard. ~ First edition.
     pages cm
  ISBN 978-0-9832944-8-1 (acid-free paper) ~ ISBN 978-0-9839346-7-7 (ebook)
  I. Title.
  PS3616.R575H45 2013
  813'.6~dc23
                                    2013007990

Please turn to the back of this book for a list of the sustaining funders of
Etruscan Press.

To Beverly Blakeslee Hiscox

Living is no laughing matter:
    You must live with great seriousness
        like a squirrel, for example —
I mean without looking for something beyond and above living,
        I mean living must be your whole occupation.

—Nazim Hikmet, "On Living" (1947)

HELP WANTED: FEMALE

Publication Acknowledgments

Slightly different versions of some of the stories in this collection were originally published in the following journals: *Green Mountains Review*: "What's Left of the Jamie Archer Band"; *New Letters*: "Two Studies in Entropy" and "The Jaws of Life" (as "Sip the Wine"); *Spittoon*: "A Forever Home"; and *The Tusculum Review*: "Help Wanted Female, Part I" (as "Help Wanted: Female"). "Two Studies in Entropy" was reprinted in the *2010 Pushcart Prize Anthology*. Thank you to the editors of these journals. The title of the story "Friends Seen and Unseen" and Prophet Zero's "transmission" on pages 83 and 84 were inspired by Prophet Omega (Omega Townsend), a radio evangelist who broadcast weekly during the 1970s, from Nashville, Tennessee, on Music Row's WNAH.

Thank you to the Silhouettes—Earl Beal, Raymond Edwards, William Horton, and Richard Lewis—for their witty and enduring number-one song from 1958, "Get A Job." Lyrics used with permission.

Lines from "On Living" from *Poems of Nazim Hikmet*, translated by Randy Blasing and Mutlu Konuk. Translation copyright © 1994, 2002 by Randy Blasing and Mutlu Konuk. Reprinted by permission of Persea Books, Inc., New York.

About the Cover Artist

CAROLINE JENNINGS is a native of rural West Virginia who has lived in Manhattan for most of the past twenty-five years while spending large blocks of time working in Europe and the Middle East. Her work is narrative in nature and strongly connected to place. For more information about Caroline's art and writing, visit her website at carolinejennings.com.

HELP WANTED: FEMALE

✦ Two Studies in Entropy ✦

To Rae-Jean's face, people said things like, "Ohmygod, thank god you're alive," or "Ohmygod, it's a miracle," or "Ohmygod, just think: *What if* you'd forgotten something? *What if* you'd gone back inside?"

What if. . . . Always, What if . . .

People would say something gruesomely speculative like that, prefaced by *What if,* and then they'd shudder and grimace in that horrible way that is almost a smile—that bizarre expression that grips people when they're relating details of life-threatening events. An expression that made Rae-Jean think of Munch's *The Scream*—the same soul-sucking posture and the same face-gripping gasp of abomination—but with a big, happy smile like Curious George.

Behind Rae-Jean's back, the same people said to each other: "Jesus, what a nincompoop!" "How stupid can a person be?" "Didn't she read the damn directions? For chrissake, there's a big friggin' warning on the label!" and "It's a wonder she didn't blow us all off the face of the earth!"

And it was a miracle. It was a true miracle that no one had been killed or maimed or even slightly injured. There was a bus stop just across the street, at the corner of Callen and Mississippi, and only moments before the blast, three junior high school boys had stood there smoking cigarettes, punching each other in the chest, and jumping up to slap and bend the street sign. A few minutes before that, Nina Summers had stood in the same spot, waiting for the Mountain Line bus.

Kids called Rae-Jean "Bombs Away Baker" and "The Flea Bomber." "Here comes (or there goes) the Flea Bomber," they'd call out every time she passed by.

Rae-Jean heard them, too. She heard them all right. They meant her to hear them. She'd never be able to live it down.

Rae-Jean was the woman who set off eighteen flea bombs in her house at 8:30 a.m. on the morning of August 27, 2002, before going to work. She was about eight blocks away, heading up Dorsey Avenue with Alice James and Ralph Waldo Emerson in the back seat, heading up to the kennel where Alice and R.W. had reservations to spend the day while the house fumigated itself. The explosion—detonated by the tiny pilot light in the furnace, no bigger than the flame of a Bic lighter—literally blew Rae-Jean's bungalow to smithereens. The windows exploded, and the front and back doors were ripped off their hinges and hurled into the alley and street. Rae-Jean's dining room wall with its built-in corner cupboard displaying her collection of carnival glass slammed through the next-door neighbor's garage. A shrapnel cocktail of glass shards, nails, and little pieces of plaster shot up high into the air like fireworks.

Five minutes after the explosion, chunks of fiberglass insulation still floated in the sky like pink clouds. 3M some of them said. 3M, R-18, R-36. Shreds of fabric—chintz, tweeds and tattersalls, corduroy, damask, black-watch plaid—pieces of upholstery, clothes, linens, old soft-bodied suitcases, and dog beds wafted about like chrysanthemum petals, coming to rest in trees and shrubbery over a mile away.

Hunks of cement from the foundation and bricks from the fireplace, buoyed up by the force and gust of the explosion, danced midair, giddy as wishing pennies atop Old Faithful.

An eyewitness on West Virginia Avenue had just stepped out of the shower when she heard the big bang. She thought it was the end of the world. She looked out her bathroom window and saw the roof of a house two streets below lifted up like the lid of a cookie jar and set back down again, as if by an invisible hand. Lifted how high? "Oh, about ten feet," the eyewitness said. She thought it was a psychedelic flashback, a little wiggle in reality. She thought she was seeing things again. She thought maybe she'd had a little stroke. She thought maybe she was on *Candid Camera.* She just didn't know what to think, she said. She got down on her knees right then and there on the bath mat—in her birthday suit—and said four Hail Marys and two Our Fathers before drying her hair.

Rae-Jean kept driving. Sure, she heard the rumble. She felt it all right. It felt like a runaway underground freight train barreling down Dorsey Hill, she said. It felt like the earth had terrible gas. In Rae-Jean's rearview mirror, the sky blossomed orange as a Japanese lantern.

What would you do? Make a U-turn? Keep going? There was a lot of commotion in the streets, in cars. It was morning rush-hour traffic. People frantically dialing their cell phones. Cars speeding up and cars slamming on brakes. Cars pulling off onto the shoulder and cars pulling up onto sidewalks. Sirens began to scream, blue and red lights to whirl and flash. One woman got out of a minivan and ran around with her arms thrown up in the air, two men chasing after her in a kind of Keystone Kops routine that reminded Rae-Jean of something people used to call a Chinese fire drill.

Rae-Jean's first thought when she heard the bang and felt the shudder and saw the orange pop-up sky behind her was: terrorist attack. But a terrorist attack on what? Walmart? Giant Eagle? Maybe the same thing was happening at the same time all over America. It never occurred to Rae-Jean that her house could be involved in any way whatsoever. Her instinct was to get away from it, whatever it was. So Rae-Jean kept driving.

At the sound of the explosion, R.W., who was startled by loud noises (even a bar of soap falling in the shower could set him off), started barking while holding his hedgehog in his mouth. This was a clever trick R.W. had taught himself years ago to muffle his bark so he could keep it up and Rae-Jean wouldn't get on his case. Employing the hedgehog mute, R.W. could carry on for sometimes as long as ten minutes before Rae-Jean got after him. The hedgehog was R.W.'s constant companion. Actually, in the name of hygiene, there were two hedgehogs, but R.W. didn't know that. He thought they were one and the same. R.W. slept with his hedgehog and kept it close by at all times, retrieving it at any barking opportunity, then barking the hedgehog-bark while keeping an eye out for Rae-Jean, calculating the extent of her patience, and then running away from the bark-inducing scene a split second before Rae-Jean was about to smack him.

Holding the hedgehog in his mouth, R.W. ran back and forth, back and forth, back and forth, back and forth across the back seat of the CRV, barking his *Mmwwoof Mmwwoof* at the mayhem, trying to make it stop. Alice James began to whimper and quiver and jumped up into the front seat, into Rae-Jean's lap, furiously licking Rae-Jean's ears and seriously interfering with her driving.

R.W. was a chocolate Lab mix. A big goofy guy the color of Duncan Hines double fudge brownie batter, with a brown nose and pinkish brown lips that looked like . . . there was no denying this: R.W.'s lips looked like night crawlers. Alice James, another rescue like R.W., was part Chihuahua and part pug. A "pughuahua," the advertisement on Petfinder.com had described her, "with maybe a little bit of rat terrier thrown in for the sake of confusion." Alice James was small and black, except for her pale, polka-dotted belly, and with disproportionately large ears like Yoda.

The day after the explosion, a very unflattering color photograph of Rae-Jean, Alice James, and R.W. appeared on the front page of the *Dominion Post* (and all over the Internet), under a hideously large head-line that shouted: WOMAN BLOWS UP HOUSE TRYING TO RID RESIDENCE OF FLEAS. The photo was taken in harsh fluorescence. Rae-Jean's face was blotchy and puffy; she looked like a criminal. In fact, she looked like both the assailant and the victim. R.W. sat slobbering on the bench beside her, hedgehog squashed in his soft, wormy mouth, and Alice James was sitting on Rae-Jean's lap, looking like a fruit bat. Alice James had a startled look on her sweet face, and her big ears stuck out like satellite dishes. Her bulgy eyes, rendered even more prominent by the camera's flash, made Rae-Jean think of poor Christina Rossetti after she'd developed Graves' disease. A very unflattering photograph indeed.

Another photo on the page-two continuation of the lead story showed the remains of Rae-Jean's house, looking like the first of the Three Little Pigs' houses—the one made out of straw—after the Big Bad Wolf had had a go at it. Still another photo showed a white clapboard

6

house with a steep green roof, a thick circle drawn around the top of the chimney. An inset to that photo — an enlargement of the circled chimney area — zoomed in on Rae-Jean's Oster toaster perched atop the chimney like a chrome Christmas tree topper.

Up until August 27, 2002, Rae-Jean had led a nice, quiet, uneventful, if boring and conventional life. She went to work every weekday. She went home. On weekends, instead of going to work, she went to Giant Eagle and Walmart and Blockbuster, and then she went home.

Rae-Jean had worked for twenty years as a copyeditor at a university press that published mostly esoteric and incoherent textbooks that it then sold for exorbitant amounts of money to destitute students who had no choice but to use their student loan money to buy these books. Rae-Jean had edited such arcane manuscripts as *The Postmodern Beowulf*, *Homosexuality and Deuteranopia in Squirrels*, *The Synthesis and Antithesis of Polypeptides*, *Freemasonry for Dummies*, and *Whither the Witch Hazel: Piles-Driven Imagery in the Poetry of Elizabeth Barrett Browning and Alfred Lord Tennyson*.

For twenty years, Rae-Jean had worked in the same dank, old building on West Virginia University's campus. Stansbury Hall was undeniably a dump, the worst building on campus, an embarrassment, an eyesore — a dilapidated, dirty brick monstrosity with a defunct gymnasium and locker room in the basement. The university press's offices — along with English, Creative Writing, Philosophy, and ROTC — were, likewise, housed in this crypt that was permeated by a peculiar and foul odor, an odor with a base note of B.O., mold, and stinky Chuck Taylors; middle notes of Lysol and something sharp and indescribable but primarily uric; and top notes of burnt Maxwell House coffee and Krispy Kreme donuts.

The press's director was a jolly little man, a foremost Samuel Pepys scholar who earned his weight times one thousand and seemed to spend a lot of time traveling to international conferences and giving basically the same paper over and over again on Samuel Pepys or spending all day in his office downloading Broadway show tunes from iTunes, which he then sang along with in a robust, off-key baritone or a hideous off-key falsetto.

Oh, I got plenty o' nuttin', you might hear him in there singing or, *Where are the simple joys of maidenhood?*

Rae-Jean's "office" was a dirty beige upholstered cubicle right outside the director's door. Sharing a cubicle with Rae-Jean—a sort of fraternal work-twin—was Wanda, the loud-mouthed public relations director with the chronic yeast infection. At least once a week, Wanda called her OB-GYN nurse practitioner to discuss her odious condition.

"Yes, cottage cheese," Wanda would say, and Rae-Jean would cover her ears and make *The Scream* face.

"Yes, yellowish . . ." Wanda would say. "Yep, fishy."

So there was all that. The ordinary twill of life; the ho-hum *sturm und drang* of the workplace: the ubiquitous absurdities, the annoying co-workers, the bloody deadlines and even bloodier bottom lines; the bland, eternal, Sisyphean, absolute, unrelenting, surreal certainty of the day-in-and-day-out of it all. Life as a slice of white bread, moistened with spit and rolled into a messy glob, a doughy ball that couldn't make the slightest dent in the iron gates of life.

But then, suddenly, on August 27, 2002, all that changed. Suddenly, Rae-Jean's uneventful life began to leaven and swell with hypotheticals. *What if* grabbed a hold of it and pumped it a few times in its death grip. *What ifs* . . . entered the picture and beefed things up a bit. *What if* Rae-Jean really *had* gone back inside?

In minutes, with the help of only eighteen Orkin flea bombs (each with a $2 mail-in rebate), Rae-Jean's little monochrome life was rendered a glorious, full-color graphic novel, each frame decorated with the words *KA-BOOM!* *BAM!* *MOMENTS LATER . . .* and *WATCH OUT!* with red and yellow starbursts all around it.

And this is only the half of it. Unbeknownst to Rae-Jean, Jamie Archer, a fifty-two-year-old homeless man, had found a home in Rae-Jean's basement and had been living there for nigh on three months. Every weekday around 10:00 a.m., two hours after Rae-Jean left for work, Jamie let himself into Rae-Jean's basement by jimmying the lock on the basement door, an entrance that was obscured by two ugly, overgrown yews and which Rae-Jean never used. Every afternoon by 3:00 p.m.—plenty of leeway before Rae-Jean returned home—Jamie let himself back out and headed downtown for dinner at the Salvation Army soup kitchen, followed by a walk along the bike trail and an evening at the library, the park, or the Friendship Room, before heading down to The Cottonwoods—the old hobo camp between the train tracks and the river, a twentysome-acre area that city law enforcement officers pretended didn't exist.

At The Cottonwoods, you could count on being left alone, at least by "the man." As long as you stayed down there all night and didn't wander up across the tracks into the edges of downtown, you were okay. You could do anything down there: get drunk, get high, get down; nobody cared. But just you stay there. There was trouble sometimes, and every year or so someone turned up dead. What happened was, now and then, somebody just got fucked up and wandered too close to the slippery riverbank and drowned, and though the *Dominion Post* always said the death was being investigated, the case was always closed the same day it opened.

One time, though, a baby turned up dead, floating in the river, and that was the only time the law ever stepped in, arresting the mother and eventually convicting her of second-degree murder. The trial was a continuing front-page story in the *Dominion Post*. And another time two sojourners known as Prophet Zero and Jesús Malverde were run over by a train, passed out on the tracks. Prophet Zero preached outside of Family Dollar, accompanied by his little dog Lucky and a group of friends known as the Family. Jesús Malverde often wore a choir robe and a string of miniature Christmas lights wound into something resembling a crown of thorns around his head. He could always be found during rush hour on the street corner by Pita Pit downtown, shouting at the traffic, waving Bob Dylan's *Highway 61 Revisited* album cover at the pedestrians and cars. Rae-Jean recognized pieces of the prologue to the *Canterbury Tales*, allusions to "The Wasteland," and lyrics from "Maggie's Farm" in Jesús Malverde's sermon as she walked by.

"*They hand you a nickel / They hand you a dime,*" Jesús Malverde would shout. "*Every fuckin' month is the cruellest month whan that Aprill, with his shoures soote / The droghte of March hath perced to the fuckin' roote. Are you having a good time?*"

After dark, the street people all disappeared back into The Cottonwoods and the abandoned warehouses and the old General Woodworking lumberyard and the condemned glass factories, and

9

the slum houses along the railroad tracks and around Stansbury Hall. From across the river, you could see their campfires burning in The Cottonwoods, and sometimes, faintly, voices and music carried across the river, but most people didn't know the old hobo camp existed.

During an eight-month period that had ended in early 2002, Jamie had actually been paid to live in someone's basement in Rae-Jean's neighborhood. A woman named Shirley Durnn was pursuing an MSW at the university and conducting a study on the movement of street people around the city. The study, entitled "Analysis and Mapping of Diurnal Migration of Transient Populations in a Mid-Atlantic, University City with a Population of Approximately 50,000, July 2001 – February 2002," was designed to evaluate the usefulness and popularity of urban social services for the homeless and to serve as a tool for planning and siting such services in comparable areas. The other principal investigator on the project was Shirley Durnn's husband, David Durnn, a geographer who had designed a geographic positioning system to map the movement of sojourners between services. The Durnn & Durnn Report, as it came to be known, was eventually published by the university press where Rae-Jean was employed and became a classic in the study of homelessness and social services, used in college classrooms across the country.

Jamie was one of twenty sojourners participating in the study. "Sojourners" was a term Shirley Durnn preferred over "homeless" because, she said, "homeless" defined a person by what they didn't have, what they were not. Sort of like the term "nonfiction." "Street person," likewise, Shirley Durnn said, was demeaning, and they should object to that title, too. Was a person who lived in a condo called a condo person? she asked.

Shirley Durnn came to the Friendship Room one evening to explain her study and its benefits for sojourners. To participate in the study, all sojourners had to do was wear a homing device—an ankle bracelet like prisoners under house arrest wear—and go about their business. No questions asked. If they completed their obligations to the study, which also included agreeing to be interviewed twice by Shirley Durnn in what she called the entrance and exit interviews, sojourners would be paid $500. Plus, sojourners would be contributing to the welfare of other sojourners by helping to evaluate services, and every sojourner would be given free housing for the duration of the study period, in the basement of "host households" around town participating in the study. Who got what basement—some were in commercial buildings, some in residences—would be determined by a lottery.

Jamie volunteered. He'd lived in basements before, once in the catacombs of a subway in another city and a few times in old university buildings on the downtown campus—the library and Stansbury Hall—and he liked all those places. But sooner or later, he was kicked out. In the lottery, Jamie drew the Durnns and was given full access to their cellar for the eight-month study period. He could come and go as he pleased, no questions asked. He had to agree to sign a contract with the Durnns saying he would not bring visitors or illegal substances to his basement digs and that he would not conduct any illicit activities there and that he would not deface any property nor smoke in bed and that he would "maintain the peace." Other than that, he could do as he pleased. Sometimes Jamie stayed away for days at a time, spending his nights and days at The Cottonwoods. Sometimes he stayed at the Durnns' for days on end, venturing out only for meals at the soup kitchens or a visit to the library.

Jamie's sojourn at the Durnns' was one of the best times of his life. David Durnn was a true dump hound. Before Jamie took possession of the Durnns' basement, David Durnn fixed it up with items neighbors had put out for the trash, which included an old office cubicle. It was beige with nubby fabric walls and had a Formica-topped desk and bookshelf with sliding doors. There was even a newspaper clipping still push-pinned to one of the fabric walls. WORKER DEAD AT DESK FOR FIVE DAYS, the headline on the yellowed newsprint said.

Jamie would have liked to have stayed there forever in the Durnns' basement, coming and going as he pleased, but when Shirley Durnns' study was complete, Shirley graduated and the Durnns moved and sold their house. Shirley tried to negotiate a provision with the realtor that the new owner would allow Jamie to continue to occupy the basement rent free for as long as he wanted, but no realtor would touch that with a ten-foot pole. When Shirley told Jamie the bad news, he cried.

Adhering to the basement-dwelling etiquette established by the Durnns, Jamie never went upstairs in Rae-Jean's house, and he never disturbed anything in the basement without returning it to its original place. When scouting the neighborhood for new digs after receiving Shirley Durnns' bad news, Jamie chose Rae-Jean's house because it reminded him of the Durnns', because it had a concealed basement entrance, and because he liked Rae-Jean's dogs. He had often walked down the alley, passing R.W. and Alice James in their fenced-in yard. R.W. always ran up to the fence, barking with a hedgehog in his mouth. Jamie would lean over the fence, R.W. would pass him the hedgehog, and Jamie would throw it a few times, which made R.W. immensely happy, and if R.W. was happy, so was Alice James, his devoted sidekick.

Every morning when he arrived at Rae-Jean's, Jamie opened the cellar door leading to the kitchen, and R.W. and Alice James came bounding downstairs. After a few games of hedgehog, rewarded by a few "street treats," Jamie unrolled his bed roll and took a long, peaceful nap behind the furnace, R.W. and Alice James curled up beside him.

Rae-Jean's house, like many houses in her working-class neighborhood, had been built by or for coal miners or glass factory workers in the first quarter of the twentieth century. Most of the houses, including Rae-Jean's, had an outside entrance to the basement, which had a crude but fully functional bathroom in one corner, complete with clawfoot bathtub.

These basements offered ideal accommodations for a sojourner. Jamie liked them. He liked the perspective—eyelevel with the crust of the earth. He liked the dirty windows, the way dust and dirt filtered the low-angled sunlight into cellars and the way smooth cement absorbed heat and light. And he liked the quietness, the guttural sounds of plumbing, the barely audible ticking of upstairs clocks, and the furnace thermostat that clicked on and off like castanets.

He liked living close to the basics—an "urban Thoreau," he thought of himself—close to the machinery that kept things going, the old well-built contraptions that kept chugging away year after year like a stout-hearted old Scandinavian farmer. He liked poured-cement floors and stone foundations, big weight-bearing posts and beams, rusty tools and ice skates hanging from pegs and 40-d nails, furnaces and hot water heaters, pipes and plumbing (especially copper and lead), dehumidifiers, washers, dryers, freezers, lawn mowers and rakes, old snow tires and snow shovels, bags of rock salt, arthritic bicycles, sleds, fishing poles, paint cans and shoe polish, odd nuts and bolts glinting from Skippy peanut butter jars, dented folding chairs, plastic bins and boxes that said things on the outside like "1985 TAXES" and "CHRISTMAS," Ball canning jars and lids, wilted amaryllises under the stairs, and dried-out geraniums hanging by their rootballs from the beams.

Jamie's favorite plant was the homely snake plant, sometimes called mother-in-law's tongue because it grew in long, sharp, tongue-like spears. Along with the Boston fern, the snake plant had been a favorite in Victorian parlors, but now snake plants, like a lot of things that have seen their day, lived mostly in basements, where they thrived on neglect. People bought snake plants on impulse and then after a few months of moving them around, grew disillusioned with them because they did nothing. But snake plants had come into their own, so to speak, in basements. They'd found a home.

Always in cellars there was running water and electrical outlets, warmth in winter, coolness in summer. Quite often there were multiple rooms: a laundry room permeated with the smell of Bounce fabric softener; a coal bin; a furnace room; a root cellar full of cobwebs and plank shelves, often with a lonely corroded jar of bread & butter pickles or tomato juice dated 1962, left behind as testimony to some former industry and abundance. One house had a secret passageway leading from the cellar to an underground bomb shelter stocked with tasty gourmet canned foods, including potted Argentinian beef, caviar, tinned cashews, and fancy apricots in heavy syrup, plus a keg of beer, cartons of cigarettes, and three cases of Spanish wine.

There was even a washer and dryer in Rae-Jean's basement, which Jamie used on an irregular basis. Plus, there were discarded things, like boxes full of books. Jamie was on page 510 of *The Postmodern Beowulf*, lost deep in the bowels of literary theory, reading an essay by some dude named Michel Foucault, who was surely tripping. Jamie was so taken by Foucault that he'd gone to the university library and "borrowed" another book by the author, entitled *Madness and Civilization*. Jamie would have legitimately checked the book out of the library, but the library made that difficult. He knew they would want things like a permanent address, a phone number, an email address, a student I.D., a passport, a driver's license—any number of positive forms of identification impossible for a sojourner to produce.

That was the problem, too, with the homeless shelters. They wanted to book you. It was the same thing with jobs. To get a job you had to have a phone number where you could be reached. To have a phone number where you could be reached, you needed a job to pay for a phone and phone service and an address to where the phone company could mail your bill.

At heart, though, Jamie was an optimist. He rolled with the flow and dodged the flow's punches. He took his chances. Without a second thought, he stuffed *Madness and Civilization* under his coat, into the back of his pants. So what if some sensible-shoed librarian caught him with Michel Foucault in his trousers? So what if some buzzer went off? Big fuckin' deal: a slap on the wrist and back out on the street sans Foucault. But if he did walk boldly, defiantly, right past that electronic eye, with *Madness and Civilization* in his pants, well then, hey, good day!

Likewise, so what if the lady who lived in "his" house came home early one day and heard the dryer rumbling downstairs and called the police? A few hours in jail, and Jamie would be run out of town—with a paid bus ticket—to another town, another basement. No big deal. No city fathers or mothers wanted to keep a sojourner in jail; they wanted to get rid of them, pass them on. They were just waiting for the perfect opportunity, looking for excuses to hand a sojourner his walking papers.

"When you got nothin', you got nothin' to lose," Jamie told Shirley Durnn during his entrance interview, when she was constructing what she called his "life narrative."

"And when you got nothin' to lose, you got everything to gain," Jamie added, smiling. "Everything you come by's a brass ring, a free ride. You find a quarter in a pay phone, and it's a prize. Trouble is, ain't so many pay phones anymore."

And when Shirley Durnn asked Jamie what it was like to have everything you own in one backpack—or, in Jamie's case, everything you own in one plaid suitcase on wheels—Jamie said it felt good, it felt like he was in control.

"When you got a lotta stuff," Jamie explained, "the stuff's got you. You gotta work to keep your stuff, and you gotta worry about your stuff all the time. You gotta worry if it's all gonna be there when you get home. You gotta worry about it because it all costs a lotta money, and it ain't paid for. You gotta work, work, work to make it work.

"The secret is," Jamie told Shirley, "you gotta not want their stuff. That's the whole secret. Not wantin' stuff. Not bein' seduced by all the stuff you see."

When Rae-Jean read the transcript of the interview with Paul James Archer, white Caucasian male, age fifty-two, who gave his address as "Bulk Mail" and his occupation as "philosopher/prophet/magician/musician," she was amazed to learn that Durnn & Durnn's background research on Archer indicated that his score on the Stanford-Binet placed him in the gifted category and that he had attended West Virginia University on an academic scholarship and had shown promise in music, language arts, and math, but then had dropped out suddenly mid-semester the second semester of his freshman year. Something had happened. Something had gone awry.

And when Shirley Durnn asked Jamie if he'd ever owned more than he did at present, more than what he had in that suitcase, Jamie said, Yes, yes he had. He'd had it all, Jamie said. He'd had a house once—a house with a mortgage—a nice house with a wall oven, a washer and dryer, and a yard—and he'd had a Plymouth once, and once a 1987 Datsun. "Good car," Jamie said. He'd even had an entertainment center once, Jamie added, laughing, and he'd had all kinds of jobs. He'd worked as a house painter and as a house carpenter and he had had his own business on the side as a handyman. He'd been in five or six bands. He'd worked as a "lumper," too. A lumper is a guy who unloads trucks for cash, he said. You just show up someplace like Giant Eagle when you know a truck's comin' in, and the driver will give you $50 cash to unload it. If you're fast, if you do a good job, then the drivers get to know you and they'll look for you among all the other lumper wannabes standing around. But if you let them down, if you don't show up a few times, you're out. Some other lumper will win their favor.

He'd worked for a bit, too, as an auto mechanic and as a taxi driver, and he'd worked for a few months at a Record Bar and for almost a year at Family Dollar, but always there'd been some kind of trouble. He'd spent some time in county jails, too. Here and there. Public intoxication. Vagrancy. Some other things that he didn't really do. "Mistaken identity," Jamie said. "Wrong place at the wrong time," Jamie said, laughing. He'd had a wife once, too, Jamie said, and two kids.

"Two boys. Two little boys. Ain't so little now, though, I suppose."

There was a long pause then when Shirley and Jamie said nothing.

"It was all too much," Jamie said.

Sometimes after work, on her way from Stansbury Hall to her car parked in the public garage downtown, Rae-Jean would pass a street person, a gangly, curly-haired, middle-aged man, leaning against a utility pole or just standing in the middle of the sidewalk reading a book, a tattered plaid suitcase on wheels beside him. The street person was always dressed in green, and Rae-Jean thought of him as the "Green Man." In spite of the fact that he was obviously a street person, Rae-Jean looked forward to seeing him everyday in his misshapen green knit hat with earflaps, his grungy green wide-wale corduroy pants, his filthy lime green sneakers, his hunter green, puffy jacket with the pointed hood, and his unraveling, olive green hobo gloves. It was part of the routine. It was like when she was a kid and went to visit her grandparents who lived in Wilkes-Barre, Pennsylvania, where Planter's Peanuts originated. All Rae-Jean and her brother wanted to do as soon as they got there was go downtown and shake hands with Mr. Peanut. Mr. Peanut was a giant peanut dressed in black tights and a black top hat and spats, and he wore the most wonderful, round-toed, incredibly shiny black shoes. He wore white gloves and carried a walking stick, and he walked around the square in downtown Wilkes-Barre all day, handing out little red-and-white-striped bags of freshly roasted peanuts. And if Mr. Peanut wasn't out, why then the whole trip was a bust, as far as Rae-Jean and Walkie were concerned.

Rae-Jean never made eye contact with the Green Man. She'd learned years ago that if you made eye contact with street people, nine chances out of ten, they'd ask you for money. At first she gave it to them: a dollar here, a dollar there, another dollar, but before she knew it, it was every day. Dollars and dollars. Word got around she was a soft-serve, and sometimes a half-dozen or so sojourners—the Rifleman, Backpack Jack, Got Any Money?, Q-Tip, Salt and Pepper, Madame Butterfly, Carwash—would be standing together on the sidewalk between Stansbury Hall and the parking garage, blocking her path, asking for money. But Rae-Jean got pissed. Wouldn't *she* like to spend the day in White Park with R.W. and Alice James instead of going to work at the university press? Wouldn't *she* like somebody to pay her way?

Rae-Jean started crossing the street to avoid the homeless people. Soon, they left her alone, and she never made eye contact with them again. Still, every time she passed the Green Man in front of the Salvation Army, she had an urge to look up, to look right into his face. Once she did, but he was reading and did not look up from his book, although she had the feeling always that his eyes were on her back once she'd passed.

No matter what the weather, the Green Man was always on the corner by the Salvation Army when Rae-Jean left work. Rae-Jean thought many times about giving him something, especially during the holidays. Maybe an envelope with a $20 bill, or maybe just a Christmas card or a little penny valentine or a prayer card, but she never did, and then suddenly he wasn't there anymore.

Since not long after "that day"—the euphemism Rae-Jean's co-workers used to refer to August 27, 2002—Rae-Jean, R.W., and Alice James had been living in an efficiency apartment on Elysian Avenue. An old woman there had died after having fallen and broken her hip, and there'd been some apartment shuffling by other tenants, leaving Rae-Jean a nice, airy flat on the bottom floor. People—good people—were always trying to give Rae-Jean things for her apartment, but secretly, Rae-Jean had developed a liking for the austerity of her new home, its sort of Japanese minimalist space. She had next to no furniture. Only three dog beds; an apartment-size refrigerator; a hot plate, and some clothes, dishes, and housewares from the Salvation Army. Pretty soon, Rae-Jean's instinct to protect her uncluttered environment took root, and she got as good at rejecting charity as she'd become at avoiding sojourners. She just said, "No. No thank you. It's too soon." Or she said she had things "on order."

There was something else about the apartment on Elysian Avenue that Rae-Jean loved: at night you could hear the train whistles and feel the furious rumble from the B&O tracks as the trains passed. The vibration from the trains made the windows in Rae-Jean's apartment chatter like wind-up false teeth, even though her apartment was blocks away from the tracks. There was a train always just around midnight, one that came flying up from Charleston, heading up toward Pittsburgh, and another one around 4:00 a.m., same direction. They were loud, all right, those trains, but not piercing and heart stopping like the fire whistles in the middle of the night, calling all volunteer firemen, or the mine whistles calling all the women, all the mothers and wives, signaling disaster. The train whistles were different. A different pitch maybe, but something about their passing gave them a different tone, a different presence, not alarming but almost benedictive. They started far away like a birdcall and then rumbled by as if delivering some benevolent message about passing and transience and life here on earth. They were regular and constant and reliable, the trains. They came and they went with the same plaintive call, the same schedule, come what may.

The trains' whistles reminded Rae-Jean of her father, who had ridden the rails as a young man. He'd lived a hard life, Raymond Walker Baker. The son of a Nebraska homesteader and one of thirteen children, he'd survived the Spanish influenza while five family members had died. As a young man, R.W. Baker made his way east during the Great Depression, riding boxcars, laboring here and there for food and shelter, moving on. At a square dance outside of Huntington, West Virginia, he'd met Rae-Jean's mother, Regina, and that was that. He settled down, took a wife. But Ray Walker always loved the trains. He watched the trains. He knew the songs: the train songs and the hobo songs. "*Hallelujah, I'm a bum,*" he taught Rae-Jean and her little brother, Walkie, to sing, "*Hallelujah, bum again / Hallelujah, give us a handout / To revive us again.*"

He knew the hieroglyphs of hobos past and had taught them to Rae-Jean and Walkie when they were kids. A circle with an "x" in the middle meant "good for a handout." A line drawing of a smiling cat meant "kindhearted lady." A rectangle with a line extending out of the top right-hand corner meant "here you can get a drink"; a box intersecting a box meant, "don't stop here." Often, as she walked R.W. and Alice James along the bike trail that followed the river, Rae-Jean studied the colorful spray-painted graffiti on the walls of the abandoned warehouses, the bridges and cliffs, thinking of her father at the kitchen table, drawing hieroglyphs on a brown paper bag. What did they mean today, the elegant swirls and alarming faces? What warnings and messages were they sending?

At night, on her dog bed, R.W. with his hedgehog and Alice James close beside her on their beds, street light and pale moonlight leaking through her blinds, Rae-Jean often lay awake, smoking a cigarette and sipping a glass of bourbon, waiting for the midnight train whistle and thinking about her father as a young man with curly dark hair, her father in dungarees and a blue light-weight cloth jacket, lying on his back in a pitch-dark boxcar years before she was born, her father, head cradled in his laced fingers, dreaming, rolling east across America, head first, rolling from the Great Plains toward West Virginia and her mother, and when she heard the rumble and whistle of the B&O trains, Rae-Jean smiled and rolled over and sighed.

After the flea bomb incident, Rae-Jean had received a large settlement from State Farm Insurance. Even though, technically, the explosion was her fault because she'd failed to adhere to the warnings of "extremely flammable" and had not extinguished all pilot lights as the small-print instructions directed, it was deemed an accident. There was a class-action lawsuit, too, against Orkin, which a young, aggressive, New York lawyer had convinced Rae-Jean to join. With the insurance money, Rae-Jean at first planned to rebuild — something small, modern, Usonian, and energy efficient — on the same lot. She'd hired an architect and worked with her for months on plans. Post-and-beam construction, tile roof, passive solar, lots of light. A Roycroft-red poured-cement floor in the main room, which would absorb sunlight and radiate heat. There was a landscape architect involved, too, and an interior decorator. A courtyard emerged; a boxwood-concealed dog run and a sophisticated, automatic, electronic dog door; a small atrium; a pantry and a walk-in closet; a terraced area with a water feature—a trickling waterfall: everything—and more—that Rae-Jean had ever dreamed of in a home. But then at some point the whole idea of building the house began to lose its appeal.

It was just too much.

After the explosion, there was a memorial service at The Cottonwoods for Jamie's suitcase. Jamie arranged it himself. He had narrowly escaped annihilation on August 27, 2002. Having arrived at Rae-Jean's house only moments before the blast, a palpable tension in the atmosphere and a terrible chemical odor made him turn and run, leaving his suitcase by the back door, and then: *KA-BOOM!* *BAM!* *MOMENTS LATER . . .*

What a story Jamie had to tell. He constructed it as a ballad. He could feel language squirming inside him like a tapeworm. He could feel words burbling up inside like he'd swallowed hydrogen peroxide. He felt giddy. "It's the blarney," his grandmother used to say when someone starting telling tales. "It's the blarney comin' out."

At the campfires that night in The Cottonwoods, Jamie roamed around and told again and again of his great escapade, telling it each time a little more fantastically. At first he said the explosion knocked him flat. In the final version Jamie told, he said he flew over the rooftops, "like an angel," for miles and miles. Over East Oak Grove Cemetery he flew, over the Gibson Brown angel and the statue of the Confederate soldier. And clear across town he glided, over the courthouse and the arboretum and over the coliseum, and then out across the Monongahela River in a big sweep, and that finally he landed on his feet in an abandoned lot full of Queen Anne's lace, out in the old Dupont Industrial Park, set down light as a feather next to a deer, set down so lightly that that doe didn't even look up or twitch an ear or flick her tail. And then he walked all the way down the River Road and across the Westover Bridge, and back into town.

That night, August 27, 2002, Jamie drank too much and smoked too much, and he wandered off to take a leak and stumbled and slid down the steep, muddy bank toward the Monongahela River. A big old button ball tree took a step sideways and leaned over, reached down a smooth white limb, scooped him up, and set him down again, safe and sound, against her trunk, and when Jamie woke up the sun was high and a tugboat named Miss Ruby was chugging by.

The Durnn & Durnn Report confirmed what Shirley Durnn had suspected all along and what any sojourner would have told her, without the services of her husband and GPS mapping. Sojourners preferred The Cottonwoods and the sheltered places underneath bridges and overpasses; the abandoned, derelict houses like "The Castle" along the railroad tracks, near Stansbury Hall, with its boarded-up doors and windows and its shredded wallpaper and missing stairs and sagging ceilings, its corroded, nonfunctional bathroom and precarious floors; and the old A&P parking garage that hung over Decker's Creek. They did not care for the regimentation and the rehabilitation that most of the social services downtown with their bright fluorescent lights and antibacterial handsoap and rules had to offer. They went to the soup kitchens for meatloaf and instant mashed potatoes and gravy and canned French-style string beans, and they went to HealthRight, and they used the bathrooms at the library . . . if it was convenient. Otherwise, they lived outside, in The Cottonwoods—like twenty-first century Indians, they said—drinking firewater, and peeing and pooping behind bushes.

A few years later, city officials, waving the Durnn & Durnn Report, succeeded in appropriating $2.5 million to bring sanitary facilities, basic utilities, and cheap weather-proof housing to The Cottonwoods. The proposed housing was one-hundred large, portable, molded plastic igloos that came in two pieces and snapped together like big dog houses. The project design also included a provision for the installation of a twelve-ft-high chain-link fence for a two-mile stretch along the B&O tracks and an iron gate that would be used to "secure" the area at nightfall.

Stating their best intentions, designers and advocates of The Cottonwoods Upgrade—as the project came to be known—described the use and condition of the century-old hobo village: it was "a narrow strip of riparian land between the B&O Railroad tracks and the Monongahela River, which had been used as a campground by vagrants since the heyday of railroads, gaining in popularity and use during the Great Depression and continuing on into the twenty-first century as more and more of the nation's indigent population took to the roads and the streets."

It was "an unsanitary and unsafe area," they said, "frequented by derelicts and public offenders." It was a "magnet for crime." It was "fouled with human waste and excrement," they said, "a breeding ground for disease and the spread of tuberculosis and other contagions." It was a "threat to nearby businesses and adjacent public property such as the rails-to-trails bike path where families recreate."

Supporters of The Cottonwoods Upgrade spoke of it as "a revitalization," as a "giant social step forward," and as a "renaissance in urban planning." Critics of The Cottonwoods Upgrade saw it as the blatant and unconscionable creation of a ghetto.

The sojourners, however, paid neither the city planners, the social workers, the construction workers, the politicians, the proponents of The Cottonwoods Upgrade, nor its opponents any mind. They simply moved up river a bit to build their fires and make their camps and construct their hives of cardboard and plastic sheeting. And from across the river at night you could still catch a whiff of smoke when the wind blew and see the campfires gleaming like tiger eyes along the riverbank, and in the skim-milky moonlight, among the sycamores and cottonwoods, the water snakes and Joe Pye, the poison ivy and touch-me-nots, hearts-a-burstin' and briery bushes, the sojourners continued to live, for the most part, outside, making do, come what may, guided only by serendipity, chance, and weather, world within world, fringe of fringe frayed, drinking the cheap, rotgut alcohol that—like its more expensive and sophisticated correlatives—takes the world away.

✦ What's Left of the Jamie Archer Band ✦

Many, many, many, many years had passed since the man with the black beard and the black ponytail and the black eyes—the man from another planet—had asked Nina to be his wife, but now that Julius was dead and buried and Nina was widowed and so alone, save for the little wire-haired fox terrier, Ponce de León, the man from another planet appeared out of nowhere—skating out of the slippery past like Chekhov's black monk—dominating Nina's imagination day in and day out in an embarrassing and some would say lascivious manner.

Nina had met the man from another planet when she was a young graduate student pursuing a master's degree in English literature and hell-bent on resurrecting from what she would eventually understand to be well-deserved obscurity a twentieth-century Southern writer with whom her mentor had had a tumultuous, illicit, all-consuming love affair in the 1950s (so he claimed) and had in his possession (so he claimed) a cache of banded letters, which he promised would rival the correspondence between Eloise and Abelard; the correspondence between Mariana Alcoforado and her French cavalry officer, Captain Noël Bouton; the correspondence between Napoleon and Josephine. These letters, the distinguished professor would share, he promised, with Nina and Nina alone if Nina would agree to base her thesis on the topic and (somewhat understood) pull down her pants.

Nina was seduced not by her thesis chairman, Dr. Chops, who was still passably handsome with grizzled hair, glinting gold crowns, a cigarette cough, and an aura of general academic debauchery, but by a postscript, the famous postscript Napoleon had added to one of his love letters to Josephine.

"I'll be there in a fortnight, my love," Napoleon scribbled as an afterthought in an 1810 letter to his beloved: "Don't bathe."

Who could decline an invitation to base their master's thesis on genuine, secret, handwritten, probably steamy and lyrical, probably perfumed love letters penned by intellectuals, instead of spending dreary hours in a musty library carrel trying to prove that Jim and Huck were up to no-good on that raft or that Virginia Woolf's lighthouse symbolized penis envy, or that all of Shakespeare's plays were written by Francis Bacon's first wife?

And, as for the pants part, Nina figured, *Hell, she could get around that.* She would see the love letters first, that was certain.

"*Semper ubi sub ubi,*" Nina said to herself, leaving the professor's dingy Stansbury Hall office. Latin for "Always Wear Underwear." It was her high school Latin club's motto, proposed by Peter Humphries, a silly, buck-toothed egghead who often wore a Boy Scout uniform to school and grew up to be a cost engineer.

After the letter-underpants proposition, Nina, full of agitated hope and promise, bids the English professor adieu and starts walking home. She walks down North High Street, past Nick's Cantina, where a greasy whiff of cheese steak makes her salivate. She crosses Wiley and continues down High, where the neon Dairy Queen sign winks and beckons to her. Nina stops, rummages in her fringed, rawhide purse for loose change. Does she have enough for a small hot fudge sundae with sprinkles? Yes!

She stands in line, waits, orders.

And just as she's at the counter window, leaning down to order, directly to her left a commotion ensues. Someone—a man—has thrown something into the large trash container beside the Dairy Queen stand, and *something* inside the can has apparently grabbed the man and pulled him in! Is it possible? The man's head and torso from the waist up are entirely inside the weighted receptacle, just his legs and Chuck Taylors protrude, kicking. A great thumping and muffled screaming resounds from inside the can.

"Help! Help!" the voice inside the trash can screams. "It's got me! It's got my arm! Let go! Let go! Help! Ohmygod, No! Nooooooooo!"

A crowd gathers. Nina drops her hot fudge sundae. Two hippies run up to the trash can, each grab a leg, and pull. Flustered and shaking, the man who was inside the trash container thanks his saviors, wipes his brow, and brushes off his tattered cutaway swallowtail tuxedo jacket. The crowd disperses, buzzing. A clump of bystanders congregates around the trash can, poking its maw with an umbrella.

The rescued man takes a step toward Nina, removes his watch cap, and bows—a deep, chivalrous, theatrical-encore bow, bending from the waist, his head touching his knees, the knit cap brushing the sidewalk with the graceful swoop of his right arm. He has a black beard and long black hair pulled back in a ponytail, and he looks a little bit like Jesus, a lot like Rasputin, and sort of like—Nina pushes the comparison out of her mind in spite of the fact that the comparison is right on: he looks a little like Charles Manson. On the sidewalk between Nina and the man who was trapped in the trash can lay the hot fudge sundae oozing from its pink dessert cup. Rising up to full height and clicking his heels, the young man with the sparkly black eyes winks at Nina and smiles. He points to the sidewalk sundae.

"My apologies," he says, motioning toward the counter. "May I . . ."

In a ginkgo tree nearby, a shiny crow with its eye on the soft-serve prize caws and flaps its wings and shifts its weight from one leg to the other and caws again, louder this time.

And so the great love affair between Nina and the man who was swallowed by the trash can—the man from another planet—begins.

When Nina first met the old woman, she was startled by her eyes: clouded over with cataracts, white as milk glass. Nina had a dish, a nesting hen made of milk glass, which her mother always said was very old and worth something. The dish belonged to Nina now, and she placed it on the Hoosier cabinet in her new garage apartment. In the hen's nest she kept the beaded hippie earrings she'd developed a weakness for.

Nina stepped on the porch and before she could knock, the screen door was pushed open by the rubber tip of a thick black cane. Had the cane been white, Nina would have put two and two together right away and realized that the old woman with her hand on the cane was blind, or nearly so. But because the cane was black, the door opening so swift, the timing so perfect—a split second before Nina's index finger pressed the doorbell—Nina did not register the cloudy eyes with anything but alarm.

Nina's grandmother had suffered from the same affliction: cataracts. Her eyes also had turned white as Orphan Annie's, but she wore glasses with smoked lenses. After some time, she'd had the operation to remove the cataracts along with the lenses the cataracts had attached themselves to like barnacles. The recovery was lengthy and involved being strapped into bed with small sandbags placed on the eyes so that the patient could not move even an angstrom in sleep, could not loll the head, roll over and jar the irises during the convalescence. The room was kept dark as a coal bin, and Nina was not allowed to enter. After the irises healed from removal of the lenses, eyeglasses had to mimic the removed lenses and were thick as paperweights. This was a common sight back then before soft contact lenses thin as cellophane, before laser surgery: old people with thick, heavy glasses that left raw sores like little heel marks on the bridges of their noses.

This all was coming back to Nina, coming down the years, as the old woman spoke.

"Come in," the old woman said. "I've been expecting you. You must be Nina."

The old woman's name was Mrs. Stella Majally, and Nina had come to Stella Majally's house to pay her deposit on the garage apartment she had rented over the phone. Stella wore a dark wool suit with a long skirt and a jacket with a large collar and covered buttons the size of nonpareils. The jacket was of good quality fabric and beautifully tailored, but it was probably at least a half-century out of style, what with its gathered shoulders; three-quarter length, puff sleeves; ribbon soutache; and empire waist. Underneath the neckline of the jacket, a few luminous pearls peeked out like the Hawkline Monster.

It did not immediately register with Nina that the ensemble was totally inappropriate for this August morning, which already promised to live up to its Dog Days' reputation, this ordinary encounter, this time—the early 1970s—this neighborhood—a student ghetto—with its rows of run-down houses built of bricks once red as strawberry jam but blackened now by time and grime, encrusted with a patina of coal dust that had turned them the color of charbroiled hamburger.

The porches of these houses, high up off the street and once flirting white gingerbread, were propped up now with unsightly, precariously leaning cinderblocks. At nearly every house a mongrel dog staked near the steps had in its restrained frenzy rendered the front yard a patch of dirt in the dry spells, mud after rain. And the lovely, decorative gingerbread, testimony to some Victorian fancy? Rotted. Peeling. Gone. And the porch steps tumbling, unsightly, tilting, descending as irrevocably as double chins.

These houses had once been the pride of immigrants—mostly eastern European—who had come to America and found work here, in West Virginia, in the glass factories along the rivers. The original houses were once neat and modest, with polished floors and woodwork, chestnut kitchen cabinets, big clawfoot bathtubs worthy of nursery rhymes and staged productions of "The Miller's Tale," and each house with an ample garden plot that extended from the back porch to the alley. Now these once-fertile gardens, planted with plum tomatoes and new potatoes and a dozen varieties of peppers, camellias, and roses—so many roses!—were thinly graveled parking lots, and most of the houses had been chopped up and converted into mean little apartments with shiny paneled walls, home to poor graduate students like Nina.

A few of the houses were still intact, inhabited by elderly people like Stella Majally, who—for one reason or another: stubbornness or economics, mostly—were holding out, refusing to sell to the absentee landlords who owned this neighborhood now, known as Sunnyside, adjacent to the university campus.

Nina had rented the garage apartment behind Stella Majally's house sight unseen, assured of its appropriateness by its classified ad description.

VERY CLEAN, ONE-BEDROOM GARAGE APARTMENT. AIRY.
WALK TO CAMPUS. $40/MONTH, INCL. UTILITIES. 292-1374.
FEMALES ONLY.

"Yes or no?" Stella Majally asked over the phone when Nina called to inquire. "I must know immediately: Do you want it? Yes or No?"

Nina hesitated. Should she commit to renting an apartment without even seeing it?

"Yes or No?" the uninflected voice asked again.

"Yes," Nina said. "Yes, yes, I'll take it." The price was, after all, right.

"Good, then," Stella Majally said. "I like your voice, and I'm tired of answering the goddamn phone."

The garage apartment wasn't exactly what Nina had in mind. What she had imagined was a small, furnished efficiency built on top of a garage. She'd been in a few such apartments about town. A creaky wooden staircase creeping up the side of an ivy-covered brick wall. One moderately good-sized room with a daybed along one wall, a gas stove, small sink, an apartment-size refrigerator squatting along the opposite wall. A few small windows. A gas heater. A tiny bathroom. A chrome dinette set, the formica-top table doubling as a desk. A plank and brick bookshelf. A moribund Swedish ivy weeping from a crude macramé plant hanger. A lumpy, overstuffed chair. A floor lamp with a scorched and lopsided pleated shade.

Not so. The apartment behind Stella Majally's house is not the second story of a garage at all. It *is* the garage, and a one-car garage at that. One whole wall is a heavy wooden garage door with a horizontal row of four little windows. The door can be opened to expose the entire living quarters and presto-change-o, drawn down again with a rope-pull. And although a hint of motor oil permeates the space, the odor is not pronounced, only suggested, and the apartment *is* clean, with new wall-to-wall indoor-outdoor carpet and plasterboard walls the color of leftover deviled eggs. A cot, Hoosier cabinet painted white and decorated with decals of cornucopias laden with colorful fruit and flowers, a sturdy but swaybacked pine table with one long drawer warped shut. Two pressed-back chairs and a round tufted ottoman. A large wicker floor lamp with an enormous woven shade like an inverted basket. A little Warm Morning gas heater. The bathroom occupies the back of the garage and is equipped with the requisite clawfoot tub, a new commode, and a sink wearing a polished-cotton skirt adorned with Bing cherries. A freshly painted white, three-legged stool.

Along the side of the garage, Nina will plant Russian Giant sunflowers, she decides, four-o'-clocks, phlox, Heavenly Blue morning glories, and hollyhocks.

It is *perfect*.

And so it is here that Nina lives and here that Nina and the man from another planet—Jamie Archer is his name—spend the night after their Dairy Queen encounter. The garage door is wide open, crickets are singing. A fog thick as cotton candy rolls in off the river, and lightning bugs prick it "like Braille," Jamie says, looking out, smiling, tickled with his simile. Coal barges moan, tugboat bells clang. Dogs bark their evensong call-and-response down the alley—*WOOF! Woof! woof!* —and now and then bursts of sparks from the enormous round chimneys of the glass factory kilns along the river splatter the night sky with spectacular, transient stars.

They were young then, Nina and Jamie, and their pasts were still interesting to them because the past had not yet become huge and incomprehensible, alien, and unmanageable, and they could dwell on the past and talk about it in the present as something logical, something cause-and-effect adding up to something that seemed to make sense. And so they reconstructed the past with ease (and embellishment, on Jamie's part), getting to know each other, eating jars of Gerber's baby food—strained apricots and split pea-and-ham junior dinners—what Nina lived off of those days—establishing each other's claim on being, pouring out the kettle of who they were, where they'd come from, what they'd done, where they'd been.

Jamie was younger than Nina, a boy really. Only nineteen. An orphan, he said.

"Sort of like a free radical," he said, laughing.

Jamie had finished school, he told Nina that first night.

"Oh, when did you graduate?" Nina asked, wondering if he meant high school or college.

"Oh, I didn't graduate," Jamie replied. "I just finished."

"Oh."

"I'm in a band now," Jamie continued. "Got my own band. The Jamie Archer Band. Got a kind of ring to it, don't you think?" Jamie said, laughing again, smiling his toothy smile.

"Close your eyes," Jamie said, and Nina heard him banging about in the kitchen corner, doing something with the oven.

"Keep them closed," Jamie instructed, untying his high-top Chuck Taylors and removing the laces.

"Okay, open your eyes," Jamie said, and Nina did, and there was Jamie standing in front of her, holding the oven rack, his shoe laces tied around the top corners. "Now, stand up," Jamie said, "and wrap the shoe laces around your index fingers and stick your fingers in your ears, and just lean forward a little bit and let the oven rack hang there, not touching your body."

"What?" Nina said, laughing, but she did as Jamie instructed. And then Jamie sat in front of her on the green Naugahyde ottoman and played the oven rack dangling from Nina's ears, played it with a spoon and a fork and a little whisk broom that he'd taken down from its hook where it hung by the door, nestled in its tin dustpan. It sounded sometimes like a dulcimer, sometimes like a xylophone, sometimes like a wind chime. And while he played the oven rack, Jamie sang, *I once had a girl/ Or should I say . . .*

What a strange, strange boy, Nina thought, her head ringing with oven-rack harmonics.

And then Jamie turned out the light and pulled from his army-issue knapsack a Fall 1970 Sears & Roebuck catalog and a red flashlight and set in to reading Nina random catalog descriptions: HOME IMPROVEMENTS (aluminum down-spouts, chain-link fencing); CRAFTSMAN POWER TOOLS (band saws, chain saws, circular saws, drill presses, routers); WOMEN'S FOUNDATIONS (girdles, bras, panties); this from the Sears Figure Control Shop, page 347:

> INFLATABLE SHORTS: Make exercise a part of your daily routine when you wear these vinyl shorts to do housework, simple exercises, or just walk! Inflated squares give pneumatic support at waist, hips, thighs, buttocks. Helps you shed body moisture, gives gentle massage. Pump and suggested exercises included. One size fits most. Weight 2 lbs. . . . $6.88.

Jamie closed the catalog and clicked off the flashlight. The garage door was wide open. The fog moved forward, the lightning bugs like infantry, some of them coming right up to Jamie's face and blinking their Morse code, as if trying to communicate, to get a better look. It was like the Battle of Cape St. Vincent, Jamie mused, when thirty-five ships passed silently within a stone's throw of the Spanish armada on St. Valentine's Day, 1797, obscured by a heavy curtain of dense, propitious fog. And Jamie lay down beside Nina and curled up against her like an inverted question mark.

Days pass. Weeks pass. Leaves fall. Jamie stays. How quickly things can change. It is that "twinkling of an eye" thing, Nina thinks. "In the twinkling of an eye we all are changed," she repeats to herself over and over. One day Nina is a serious graduate student, unattached, and then suddenly, over a spilt hot-fudge sundae, she is in love, cohabitating, staying up into all hours of the night reading *A Coney Island of the Mind* and *Reality Sandwiches* aloud and listening to *Tea for the Tillerman* and *The Dark Side of the Moon*, over and over and over again, dancing in her underpants, making love, not war.

Eventually, the sunflowers droop but the stalks remain standing along the garage wall like a long row of locker room showers. Jack Frost scribbles his crazy poetry on the four little garage windows, the blue flames on the gas stove dance, the Warm Morning heater glows rosy red, and Jamie and Nina stay under the covers, cuddling while the wind whistles through the joints in the wooden garage door, and snow piles up in big, elegant swoops and drifts along the alley.

They are in love, Jamie and Nina—so Nina thinks—but after awhile, things are not going well. One day Nina trudges home through the snow after teaching—she has a graduate teaching assistantship and teaches two sections of a freshman-level writing class called Composition & Rhetoric, even though, if pressed for a definition, she's not really sure she could tell you what rhetoric really is—and Jamie and two of his friends are sitting in the garage apartment, huddled around the Warm Morning heater, smoking pot.

"You don't mind if they stay, do you, Nina?" Jamie whispers to Nina. He is referring to Trapper Bill and Simon Magus, his two band members who have been living in tents along the river, in an old hobo camp known as The Cottonwoods and who have begun to appear at Nina's garage apartment more and more often. Every day, to be exact. The temperature is supposed to drop that night into the low teens, and what can Nina say? Trapper Bill has already pitched his pup tent outside the bathroom, and under the table, Simon Magus has unrolled his sleeping bag, a tattered olive-green affair lined with a flannel of mallard ducks frozen in flight.

Even though Jamie talks often of his band and their big break, Nina has no idea what kind of band it is, and they never have had any gigs, as far as Nina can tell. And there seem to be no instruments save a tambourine, which Simon Magus always carries, tapping it against his thigh, and a plastic flutophone that Jamie plays. Finally, Nina asks.

"Madrigal," Jamie says. "Madrigal singers."

Simon Magus's real name is Henry, Jamie tells Nina, confidentially, "but don't ever call him that." Jamie whispers. "Call him Simon. Or Merlin."

Simon is a sweet, elfish character with curly ash blond hair and burning eyes, who claims he can fly and levitate objects. Once he convinces Nina to be levitated. They light candles and strawberry incense and Nina lies on the wooden table in a flannel nightgown, and Simon dances around the table, chanting and shaking his tambourine and waving a sage smudge stick, while Jamie plays his flutophone and Trapper Bill strums the oven rack with Nina's whisk broom. Nina feels a strange twitching and tingling along her spine and a little breeze tickling its way up under her nightgown, and according to Jamie and Trapper Bill and Simon Magus, her body hovers a few inches above the table and glows. Simon declares that Nina is a reincarnation of Helen of Troy, and from then on, whenever Jamie or Simon or Trapper Bill greet her, they say, laughing, "Is this the face that launched a thousand ships?"

Nina begins to spend more and more time at the library and in her "office" in Stansbury Hall: a dank, windowless basement space she shares with five other graduate teaching assistants. She leaves the garage apartment early in the morning while Jamie and Simon and Trapper Bill are still sleeping and comes home after dark, usually to find the Three Musketeers (which is what she calls them) sitting on the floor, in front of the Warm Morning heater, stoned, and discussing Nostradamus or Zarathustra or reading aloud random passages from *Finnegan's Wake* or "The Wasteland" and playing "Revolution Number 9" backward on Nina's record player.

Paul is dead. Paul is dead, a spooky, scratchy voice intones.

Often, they have prepared a meal: one time, squirrel, which Trapper Bill has trapped in the university's arboretum, and another time, stone soup: a murky broth with carrots and gravel—which Simon explains he has rinsed and boiled to sterilize and which contains rich trace minerals and one-hundred percent of the recommended daily allowance for calcium. You are supposed to suck on the gravel and spit it out, of course, Simon Magus instructs. Nina eats nothing those nights.

And on top of that, progress on Nina's thesis is going slowly. Actually, not at all. She's gotten the letters from Dr. Chops, and they are nothing like she had hoped. They do not illuminate one single interesting thing about the quasi-famous Southern writer, and furthermore, they reveal the quasi-famous Southern writer to be rather trite and affected, a very poor speller, and ignorant of the proper use of semicolons. The letters are boring, full of smarmy endearments, their very existence an embarrassment. Nina begins to feel pity for Dr. Chops, who has saved this banal correspondence for so many years and put so much stock in it. Slowly, Dr. Chops takes on an old and weary appearance, and Nina is mortified to see him. She writes nothing that semester—not a single word on her thesis—and she cancels every appointment with Dr. Chops, leaving vague notes in his mailbox, claiming fever, impacted wisdom teeth, migraine headache, mono, food poisoning, hives, female problems, and a death in the family.

One bitter February morning—Valentine's Day, to be exact—leaving the garage apartment for school, Nina steps out into the alley, and Stella Majally calls to her from her back porch. Stella is wearing a large fur hat like a Cossack's and a heavy fur coat, which upon closer inspection, appears to be ancient seal or ratty sheared beaver.

"Nina! Nina!" she calls, "I must speak with you."

Nina has only twenty minutes to get to Armstrong Hall before her class begins, but she hurries up the walk and climbs the slippery stairs to Stella Majally's back porch.

Mrs. Majally ushers her inside.

"Who are they?" Stella wants to know, and, "Where did they come from?" and, "Are they living with you?" She is stern with Nina. She reminds Nina that the lease she signed stipulates *females only* and that there is a provision that no overnight guests are allowed. Nina bursts into tears. It is all too much. She wants them gone, too, but how will she tell them?

"You just tell them to leave, dear," Stella instructs, "or I'll call the police."

All that day, Nina frets over the inevitable confrontation with Jamie and his band members. If only Simon Magus and Trapper Bill would leave, and she and Jamie could be alone again, but even then, Stella Majally would not approve. And lately, Jamie seems agitated and hyperactive. He talks endlessly, long into the night, espousing all kinds of crackpot theories and wild ideas. He believes in spontaneous generation and is going to get a government grant for $50,000 to prove it, he says, and his only investment will be a box of Rice Krispies. And he says that in a lucid dream the true location of the Fountain of Youth has been revealed to him by heavenly beings—he alone has been given the coordinates and has written them in indelible ink on his ankle; the Fountain of Youth is at N41° 14.6281', W075° 53.558', underneath a building infested with fleas and bats.

And he says that the philosopher's stone is not a stone at all but a medium: Jell-O pudding and pie filling. The garage apartment is full of boxes of Jell-O, which Jamie simmers day and night, adding coins and nuts and bolts and flatware, trying to convert base metals into gold. It is the aluminum stew pot, Jamie declares, that is inhibiting the transmutation, and so they save S&H green stamps, pasting them in their flimsy little books, saving up for a enameled graniteware canning contraption, which Jamie is certain will do the trick. Jamie's beard grows longer, his eyes brighter. He has stopped bathing and washing his hair and insists that they sleep with the garage door wide open, even though the night temperatures drop to well below freezing.

For a Valentine's Day present, Nina has bought Jamie a wooden recorder, which he has often admired in the window of DeVincent's music store. The recorder is a beautiful dark cherry with its own small, velveteen-lined cedar box and a soft piece of blue cotton flannel and a rod for cleaning and a rolled paper displaying a fingering chart and the music to "Sailor's Hornpipe" and "Greensleeves." Nina bought it on layaway for $35, paying $5 per week, and has kept it in her office, hidden in a desk drawer, wrapped in aluminum foil and tied with a satin hair ribbon. They have arranged to meet in Sunnyside at a bar called the Bon Ton Roulette, which is decorated with hats. Nina has saved sixteen dollars, more than enough to buy them one cheeseburger and french fries platter and two mugs of beer each. Provided that Trapper Bill and Simon Magus don't show up, that is.

The Bon Ton Roulette is a dark, semi-subterranean tavern in an alley, two blocks up from the river, down a flight of stone steps, with a heavy plank door and a sticky, slate floor. Wooden booths line the knotty pine walls, and small candles flicker on the tables. The room is crowded and noisy, full of college students, young lovers. Bob Dylan is singing "Visions of Johanna," and Nina spots Jamie in a booth in the corner near the door, under a mobile of men's fedoras, a stained glass window depicting Adam and Eve behind him. Nina's heart flutters. Thank god, Simon Magus and Trapper Bill aren't with him. But how will she tell Jamie that even though she loves him, she's kind of afraid of him, and she wants her old life and her garage apartment back?

Jamie jumps up and embraces her and pulls her down beside him. "Is this the face that launched a thousand ships?" he says and kisses her forehead. Nina pulls off her velvet beret.

In his hand, Jamie conceals a tiny box, a midnight blue sueded box, and inside it, swaddled in white satin, is a ring. A mood ring. And Jamie proposes.

"Nina," he says, "Nina, I love you. Nina, will you be my wife?"

Nina is dumbfounded.

And Jamie continues his declaration of love. He will honor Nina and adore her, he says. "For rich or for poor," Jamie says. "In sickness and in health," Jamie says. "From this day forth, even forevermore." And then he adds that there is one thing he must tell her. He will mention it now, Jamie says, but it will never have to come up again, never be an issue, but he must tell her. He must be honest and up-front as they embark on their life of marital bliss.

"I'm from another planet," Jamie tells Nina, "but in this life I am just like you. I am *exactly* like you. I, too, am a spiritual being on a human journey. And my origins will make no difference to our life together. I am human incarnate just like you, do you understand, Nina?" Jamie says, his eyes blazing. "But when I die, my spirit will return to my planet. I just wanted you to know, Nina, my love."

That was long ago. Nearly forty years ago when Nina ran out of the Bon Ton Roulette alone and stayed in her office for five days, afraid to go home. And when she did go, accompanied by a friend, no sign of Jamie and his band remained. Even the Jell-O pudding and pie filling boxes were gone. The only evidence of Jamie having been there was a flimsy book of S&H green stamps, all but two rows of the last page full, laid atop her *American Heritage Dictionary*, which always sat on the Hoosier cabinet, next to the milk glass nesting hen.

And the oven rack was gone.

And Nina never saw Jamie Archer or Simon Magus or Trapper Bill—or her oven rack, for that matter—again.

Time passes, and Nina gives up on her love-letter thesis chaired by Dr. Chops and drops out of graduate school and takes a job as a technical writer for a contractor to the Department of Energy and at age thirty-three marries a dull but responsible cost engineer, who is known in the workplace and their social circle for his puns, and after every pun he says, "No pun intended, ha-ha-ha-ha." But Julius is a good man, a good husband, a good father, a good provider, and Nina raises three dull and responsible children, punsters all, and Nina has always hated puns, and over the years, she forgets all about Jamie Archer and his mood ring and his band and Simon Magus and Trapper Bill, and settles into her ordinary life, except for now and then when she reaches for her 1970 *American Heritage Dictionary* and out falls a book of S&H green stamps.

The little garage apartment is gone now, along with the Russian Giant sunflowers, the four-o'-clocks, phlox, Heavenly Blue morning glories, and hollyhocks, as well as Stella Majally and her red-brick house and pretty much the entire neighborhood.

Where Nina's garage apartment once stood are stacked row upon row upon row of cheap, prefabricated townhouses. "The Kennels," Nina calls them. She drives along Beechurst Avenue, shaking her head in disapproval, Ponce de León riding shotgun, his front feet on the dashboard, yipping at everything that moves or appears to be moving, which is, of course, everything. The glass factories, too, are gone, and the immigrants who worked in them. One factory—Bailey Glass—is a honeycomb of chichi shops that sell Birkenstock shoes and Crabtree & Evelyn soaps, Ruffoni and Le Creuset cookware, expensive wines, and Swarovski crystals, antique glass-blowing instruments decorating the brick walls.

One day Nina is out driving with Ponce de León, headed for her monthly oncology check-up, and she stops at a stoplight in Sunnyside, and there, right beyond her car is a poster stapled to a utility pole. WHAT'S LEFT OF THE JAMIE ARCHER BAND, the poster says, Saturday, August 4, 10:00 p.m., 123 Pleasant Street. Nina throws her Mini Cooper into park, jumps out and rips down the sign, Ponce de León barking wildly.

It's only Tuesday, and Nina looks at the torn poster day and night. She is sixty-two years old and has osteoporosis, hypothyroidism, hypertension, low blood sugar, high cholesterol, a weak heart, free-floating anxiety, plantar fasciitis, osteoarthritis, and only one breast. Julius has been dead for seven years. Nina had been to 123 Pleasant Street many years ago, when it was a hippie bar called The Underground Railroad and Bo Diddley played there and it was operated by a woman named Marsha Mudd, who disappeared in 1988. Some people say Marsha Mudd was murdered, some people say she had ties to the Chicago Seven and has gone underground; some people say she was a drug informant and now lives under an assumed identity in a foreign country but had been spotted dancing wildly at a Grateful Dead concert years later in Golden Gate Park. Some people say Marsha Mudd has gone to the planet where Jimi Hendrix, Janice Joplin, and Jim Morrison were really from and have returned to.

Tuesday, Wednesday, Thursday, Friday. Saturday, August 4, 2010. All day and every night since she came upon the poster, Nina thinks of Jamie. In bed at night, she dreams of the garage apartment and the little army cot, and she can almost feel Jamie curled against her, his breath on her neck. But it is only Ponce de León. Maybe Jamie has found it: the Fountain of Youth. Maybe he has transmuted base metal to gold. Maybe he has gone back to his planet? Will Jamie be there at 123 Pleasant Street with his flutophone or Nina's oven rack and a Sears catalog or the recorder still wrapped in its tinfoil and tied with its satin bow, which Nina left on the seat of the booth at the Bon Ton Roulette so many years ago? Will Simon Magus be there? Trapper Bill? Would she recognize any of them? Would they recognize Helen of Troy at age sixty-two? The face that sunk a thousand ships?

Six o'clock. Seven o'clock. Eight o'clock. Nine. Ten o'clock. Eleven. Nina is parking her car under a security light in the municipal parking garage across from 123 Pleasant Street. A bunch of terribly young, terribly dangerous-looking people with tattoos and dreadlocks and mohawks and pierced lips and noses, and earlobes stretched down to their shoulders, wearing torn clothing and studded dog collars and sneers, are standing outside smoking, and Nina walks in, wearing her Eva Gabor wig and her lavender polyester slacks and penny loafers and her navy blue L.L. Bean all-weather parka. It's dark inside and a deafening-loud band is playing, the lead singer shouting words Nina can't understand and flicking his head like his neck is broken. The bass vibrates through the floor and rattles the bottles and glasses behind the bar.

In her coat pocket, Nina has the tattered poster advertising WHAT'S LEFT OF THE JAMIE ARCHER BAND. She hands it to a person with a shaved head and tattooed face—is it male or female?—standing inside the door, collecting the cover charge. She-he looks at it, expressionless, and hands it back to Nina, never making eye contact but pointing to a chalkboard on the wall that says $10 cover and the names of five bands:

1.   Jerry Falwell and The Panty Liners
2.   Urban Couch
3.   Gene Pool
4.   63 Eyes
5.   Non-Dairy Creamer

"But what about this?" Nina shouts above the noise, pointing to her poster. Queequeg doesn't acknowledge that Nina has spoken. Nina waits, invisible, and when all the punk-rock patrons have entered, she pays her $10 and stands against the wall, by the door, in her thin jacket, feeling like an alien, until last call.

Now it is late, after 3:00 a.m., and the streets of Morgantown are deserted and slick-shiny from a sudden rain, but the storm is over and the sky is pocked with stars. Nina's car is the only car in the parking garage, which smells like piss. Nina walks toward the car, her ears ringing, feeling sick with the cling of cigarette smoke. At least her car is under a security light. In the lee of the garage, in a dark corner, something shifts, something moves, and Nina, startled, fumbles for her keys, her heart pounding. Safe inside her little Mini Cooper, she quickly locks the doors and turns the key in the ignition. She backs out, and heading toward the exit, her headlights illuminate the dark corner. It is a human form, a man. Someone pulling a bright green tarp over his head. He must be wearing a backpack because underneath the tarp, it looks like he has wings, and Nina is reminded of the famous gargoyle perched atop Notre Dame Cathedral. It is probably the street person everyone refers to as the Green Man, a man with a long grizzled beard, always dressed in green, who is usually stationed downtown, outside the Salvation Army, staring blankly at the traffic or reading.

Something about seeing the Green Man makes Nina feel strangely, buoyantly happy. As if he is a tiny flag, push-pinned on a wall map, something familiar and reliable. Something that says YOU ARE HERE or YOU ARE NOT ALONE.

How silly of her, she thinks now, to have thought that Jamie and some of his band members might be there tonight. But where did that poster come from? Was it some kind of sign Jamie was trying to send her? Was he really from another planet? And why not? She has read Carl Sagan. She knows about SETI, the Search for Extra-Terrestrial Intelligence. Life is random, the possibility of intelligent life existing *only* on planet Earth, ridiculous. And, furthermore, is this life form really so intelligent? Think about it.

What does it mean to be human? Nina asks herself, driving the few blocks home. Is it being a biped with opposable thumbs and a big brain? Is it membership in a certain class and phylum/order/family/genus/species? Is it something a saliva test can ascertain? Is it some set of attributes and attendant behaviors: ten of these, two of those, one of that? Is it something you can draw a box around? Who are we, anyway, and where did we all come from, and just what . . . what . . . what on earth are we doing here?

As always when Nina's been gone, Ponce de León has been standing on his hind legs, his front feet on the window sill, keeping vigil, watching out the kitchen window, guarding the den and listening for Nina's little car to swing into the alley. In the beam of the porch's amber bug light, his sweet little face looks sad and tired, wizened and jaundiced, and oh so old. He'll be ten come spring, seventy in human years. In a few years, he'll be dead. And what about Nina? What will be the measure of her days, her inch or two of time? It's way past Ponce de León's bedtime, but he's still awake, waiting faithfully for Nina to return. He is all she has, really. She is everything to him. He paws at the window and smiles and jumps for joy. A catbird meows from the yews as Nina swings open the garden gate and one errant shooting star rips through the lining of the moth-eaten night.

+ The Jaws of Life +

Her name was Sissy and she was coming to clean the house, and according to Abigail's friend Deborah, who was a social worker, Abigail would be doing this poor woman a favor by letting her clean her house.

Sissy had a learning disability and many hardships, Deborah said. She was widowed. Her husband—an abusive sort, a drinker—had done under-the-table odd jobs all his life, so there was no pension, no health insurance, no benefits of any kind, no money coming in. He'd done some time in prison, too, for second-degree murder, Deborah said, but it was really self-defense, and he'd served only half his sentence, having been released early for good behavior. Anyway, he was dead now.

He died under suspicious circumstances, but there was no investigation. "You know how that goes," Deborah said matter-of-factly.

Sissy had worked in Food Services at the university for many years. She had a good work record, but she'd been laid off during the recent state cutbacks that left over two hundred minimum-wage workers unemployed and the new president—an old friend of the governor's daughter (who, herself, was CFO of a behemoth pharmaceutical company owned by an alumnus of the university, who just happened to be the university's biggest donor)—earning an annual income of probably half a million dollars, plus a rent-free mansion and who-knew-what-all benefits and perks. Not nearly as much as the football coach, but still, nothing to sneeze at.

Yes, times were hard all right, but Sissy was a survivor. Her unemployment—little that it had been—had run out. She was trying to get back on her feet, get off welfare, and make a living by cleaning houses. She lived in Osage, Deborah said.

Osage was a poor, run-down area north of town, a shantytown along the railroad tracks and the river, a community plagued by neglect and crime, a place immortalized by Walker Evans in his 1930s photographs documenting the lives of the Appalachian poor. Sissy had references, Deborah said, from the university's Human Resources Department and the social services agency. She was a good person, a very hard worker, just a little slow. She'd had a tough life. A stereotypical, West Virginia backwoods life: no education to speak of, married young, too many kids, years of poverty and isolation and abuse. But she was honest and reliable and trustworthy. Wouldn't Abigail give her a chance? Please? Just once, let her try? Abigail could make a difference in Sissy's life. And if it didn't work out, why there was no commitment.

What could Abigail say?

"Great!" Deborah chirped when Abigail agreed, "You won't regret it, Abby. I'll make all the arrangements."

Sissy would come to Abigail's house on Saturday at 9:00 a.m., three days away. Abigail would be home and could show Sissy what needed to be done. It was all set. Agreed upon.

A cleaning lady? Abigail thought when she set down the phone, *Me, with a cleaning lady?* She was a bit peeved at Deborah for talking her into one. Abigail really didn't want anybody cleaning her house. She was a neat person, a fussy person. She cleaned her house herself, every day. A place for everything, and everything in its place. She'd lived alone for twelve years. She was in control of her life. She had a good job, and she owned a neat little 1920s brick bungalow in a good neighborhood, a Sears house that she'd bought at a good price and a low interest rate, and which she had carefully remodeled little by little over the years with new windows and tasteful wallpaper, adding Ethan Allan furniture and Oriental accent rugs for her hardwood floors. She subscribed to *Dwell, Interior Design*, and *Real Simple*. Recently, she'd had the yard landscaped, adding a flagstone patio, a dog run, and a modest water feature. Abigail didn't want somebody coming into her house and hovering about, touching and moving her things. She didn't need a cleaning lady. She was more than a little bit peeved at Deborah for talking her into one.

There had been men in Abigail's life—years ago—but in the end, they all seemed lacking and ineffectual, even Frank McDonough, whom she'd lived with for almost six years. At first, after Frank left, she missed the companionship and occasional sex, but gradually she began to realize that really there were only two things she liked to do in bed: sleep and read. Well, three, maybe: sometimes she liked to eat in bed. Indian (saag paneer) or Chinese (mu-shu vegetable) take-out, while she read. Then she got a dog—a little Welsh terrier—and life sweetened. Richard Burton slept on the bed, and Abigail read long into the night, his warm little body nuzzled against her. He was all she needed.

Abigail had worked as a cleaning lady herself years ago in a little town on an island on the Outer Banks of North Carolina. It was the summer of 1969, and she was in college then. She'd gone to the beach for the summer with one of her college roommates, Sherry. They were going to get waitressing jobs and sexy, golden tans, but when they arrived at the resort town, there was only one waitressing position left on the whole island—at the Pony Island Restaurant, where the waitresses wore hot pants and cowboy boots and fringed halter tops and ten-gallon hats, and the waiters wore chaps and bolo ties and cowboy boots and ten-gallon hats, and Sherry—who looked like Tuesday Weld—got that job. Abigail, who had been asked more than once when she was young if she were related to Don Knotts, was offered a housekeeping job at the adjoining motel.

The housekeeping staff at the Pony Island Motel wore dumpy hunter green sack-like polyester dresses with long steel zippers up the front and dingy pinafores, the pockets stuffed with complimentary packets of Nescafé coffee, Sanka, Tetley tea, Sweet & Low, and Domino sugar. For five or six hours every day, Abigail pushed around a galvanized steel wash bucket on wheels, complete with a sour, mangy mop, and a caddy with cans of Lysol and Pledge, an industrial-size bottle of Pinesol, another of Windex, an old brown plastic toilet brush like a beaver's tail, and a wad of stiff pink rags. The first week of work, Abigail developed a rash from the cleaning products, and her skin began to itch and peel. The itching and peeling started slowly between her fingers, then spread like kudzu to her palms and up her arms, across her torso, up her neck and chin and onto her face. The rash lasted all summer, and she had to stay out of the sun, which only exacerbated the scaling and itching.

She got up at 7:00 a.m. six days a week that summer and rode her bike to the Pony Island Motel office where she was paired with an enormous, slovenly, chain-smoking veteran cleaning woman named Goldie, who smelled like garbage and carried around a large plastic *Happy Days* cup of ice, half-filled with Coca-Cola, to which she added a splash of booze from any open liquor bottles that could be found in any of the vacated rooms as she and Abigail made their way along the rows of numbered doors. Vodka, tequila, rum, gin, brandy, Scotch, amaretto, sherry, vermouth, triple sec, crème de menthe—whatever was open, Goldie added a splash to her cup. By 8:00 a.m., Goldie was sloshed on the ultimate Long Island Ice Tea. She drug around a battered, twenty-five-pound Electrolux vacuum cleaner with a gimp wheel, like a drunk toddler with a pull toy, and stumbled into each room, crashing into things, knocking over lamps and open suitcases, and eventually landing in or near the ubiquitous mustard-colored vinyl arm chair where she snoozed while Abigail changed the sheets, gathered the dirty towels, scrubbed the bathrooms, vacuumed, and dusted. Before passing out, Goldie pocketed all the tips laid out on the bureau tops.

The second week of work, Goldie tripped over the Electrolux—which Abigail had named Cleo after the talking basset hound on *The People's Choice*, an old Jackie Cooper sitcom from the late 1950s. Cleo's inertia reel cord jerked out of the hall socket and lashed out like a cobra, whipping Abigail in the face as it spun and recoiled back into the Electrolux's belly. The accident sent Cleo speeding along the cement second-story corridor of the Pony Island Motel like a torpedo, flying off the iron staircase and landing in the parking lot, where she crossed the path of a Dominion Hope power truck backing up. Abigail cheered at the impact, but amazingly, Cleo was unharmed. (You had to hand it to those Swedes!) Goldie sprained her ankle.

By mid-summer, Abigail was carrying a gigantic *Happy Days* cup half filled with ice and Coca-Cola around the Pony Island Motel, too.

Friday night, Abigail straightened and primped her house so it would look nice for Sissy, the new cleaning lady.

A little before 6:00 a.m. on Saturday, Richard Burton started barking his alarm bark and racing up and down the stairs. *Somebody's on the front porch, somebody's on the front porch, somebody's on the front porch, coming to kill us, coming to kill us, coming to kill us dead.* Abigail threw on her kimono, headed downstairs, and opened the front door. A woman of indeterminate age stood there. She could have been thirty or forty or even fifty. Who could tell with all that makeup? She had a horsey face and long squirrel-colored hair pulled back severely into a stringy ponytail fastened with some kind of clasp adorned with what looked like furry orange and green ping-pong balls.

"Miss Shapiro, I come to clean your house," Sissy announced flatly as Abigail opened the door.

"I thought you were coming at nine?" Abigail said wearily as Sissy pushed past her.

"What time is it now?" Sissy asked.

"It's not even six," Abigail said, "6:00 a.m." It was barely light. The street was empty. The street lights were still on. The morning paper had not yet been delivered. Birds were still snoring and dreaming in their nests.

Sissy wore a faded denim wraparound skirt with a sad likeness of a unicorn poorly embroidered on the front, its horn like an enormous wilted carrot, and an ugly yellow Donkey Kong t-shirt. From one shoulder dangled a dirty pink plastic My Little Pony backpack. *Well,* Abigail thought to herself, taking in this fashion statement, *I guess there's an attempt at coordination: an equine theme.*

Abigail looked out at the driveway, which was empty. "How did you get here?" she asked Sissy.

"I walked," Sissy said. "Where should I start? Do ya have anything to eat? This sure is a steep hill. I could utilize a cup of coffee."

Walked? Abigail thought to herself. *Good gawd!* Osage was at least six or seven miles away.

Abigail led Sissy into the kitchen and began making a pot of coffee. "Do ya have a bathroom?" Sissy asked, and Abigail directed her to the stairs. Sissy was gone for what seemed like a mighty long time. The coffee had finished its little rumba, and in the silence, Abigail thought she heard the shower running. At least fifteen minutes must have passed before Sissy descended the stairs in her bare feet with one of Abigail's Laura Ashley towels wrapped around her head. Her face looked red and raw, as if it had been scrubbed with the Ajax Abigail kept under the sink, but she had on lipstick. Lipstick that looked to be the exact color that Abigail wore—Mary Kay Amber Suede—which she kept in a cut-glass dish on the bathroom vanity.

Dumbfounded, Abigail handed Sissy a mug of coffee. Richard Burton sniffed Sissy's big hammer toes and growled.

"Cream and sugar?" Abigail asked.

"Yes," said Sissy, "and eggs. I'd like some eggs. Scrambled eggs. And toast. With jelly. Grape jelly. Bacon, if ya got it. And grits. Nice place ya got here, Miss Shapiro. Do ya live alone? How much did that fancy toaster cost? Is that a genuine Mr. Coffee?"

Abigail didn't answer. She cracked the eggs and whisked them in a Fiestaware bowl.

The bacon sizzled. The toast popped.

Sissy wolfed down her breakfast before Abigail even sat down and then unabashedly announced that she was still hungry. Could she have more?

Eight eggs, four pieces of toast, and a half-pound of bacon later, Sissy pushed her plate away and put her head on the table. The towel fell off her wet head onto the plate.

"Is something wrong, Sissy?" Abigail asked, yawning.

"I feel sick," Sissy moaned. "I got me one of them my-grained headaches. It could be a brain tumor. I feel like I'm dying. I need to lay down."

"Of course," Abigail said, leading the way to the living room, fluffing the throw pillows on the sofa, and unfolding the afghan. But when Abigail turned around, Sissy was gone. She was headed back upstairs.

Abigail sat on the next-to-bottom step, tickling Richard Burton's belly, and waited. Had Sissy gone up to use the bathroom? Minutes passed, this time without the sound of running water or a flushing toilet.

"Sissy?" Abigail called softly up the stairs. "Sissy?"

Nothing.

"Sissy?" a little louder. "Sissy?"

Abigail tiptoed up the stairs. Her bedroom door was partially closed, and there was Sissy asleep in Abigail's bed, the Donkey Kong t-shirt, the hideous denim skirt, and something incongruous—something black and lacy—in a tangled heap on the floor.

During that summer of 1969, when Abigail worked at the Pony Island Motel, she and her roommate Sherry grew further and further apart as the days and weeks passed. Sherry went out after work every night with the other cowgirls and cowboys from the restaurant and had taken up with a waiter named Livingston, who lived in a tent in the national park campground and played the guitar. She hardly ever came back to the boarding house where she and Abigail shared a room. Only to shower and change her clothes.

Somehow, Abigail started spending the evenings with Goldie and her husband, Big Willard, out on "the Flats," drinking plonk and eating fried mullet and greasy collard greens seasoned with fatback, munching on bags of cheese curls and barbequed pork rinds, and watching *Hee-Haw*.

Big Willard owned the only garbage-collection service on the island, and when not in use, the stinky garbage truck was always parked in front of Big Willard and Goldie's trailer. The stench of rancid garbage wafted through the screens and clung to Abigail's hair and clothes. It had permeated the upholstery, the shag carpet, the draperies, the paneling and linoleum, the *National Enquirers* and *Soap Opera Digests* littered about Goldie and Big Willard's trailer. Even the inside of Goldie and Big Willard's refrigerator smelled like garbage, but like everything else in life, you just got used to it.

Big Willard had had his leg amputated because of diabetic neuropathy—"the sugar," they called it. "Poor Willard, he's got the sugar," Goldie told Abigail. Goldie and Willard's son, Little Willard, was five years older than Abigail and had taken over his father's garbage collection business. Little Willard was tall and lanky, with ropey arms and a Bugs Bunny tattoo on one bicep. Under the tattoo, it said, WHATS UP DOC? without any punctuation except the question mark. For some reason, this absence of punctuation annoyed Abigail to no end, and she often had the greatest urge to take a ball-point pen and ink in the missing apostrophe and comma.

The tattoo, Little Willard explained without prompting, was for his son, Willard the Third, known as Doc. Doc was six and lived with Little Willard. Doc's mother—Little Willard's wife—had run off with a tourist on Memorial Day. It wasn't the first time she'd run off. It was the third or maybe the fourth—Little Willard wasn't sure. There was one time when she was gone only one night, so he didn't know whether to really count that time or not.

If she came back this time, would Little Willard take her back? Abigail asked.

"Oh, yeah, probably . . . yeah," Little Willard said, laughing. She was a wild thing, he said, "Angel is *wild*." She couldn't help herself, he said, but she loved him and Doc. Maybe she'd outgrow it—the wildness—Little Willard said, but that's what he loved about her. He called her his "Wild Angel."

Little Willard was known locally as a creative thinker and clever businessman. He had instituted the practice of collecting the garbage at night—when it wasn't hot—so he could go surfing during the day. He started out about 8:30 p.m. every night and worked until at least midnight, sometimes later, driving the truck and picking up the garbage himself. It wasn't long before Abigail was leaving Goldie and Big Willard's in the middle of *Hee-Haw* and riding along with Little Willard on his garbage route, Doc asleep on the bench seat between them. And it wasn't long after that when Doc started sleeping at Goldie and Big Willard's while Abigail and Little Willard drove around the quiet streets alone, smoking pot and drinking wine from a jug on the floor, listening to mix tapes: The Doors. The Beach Boys. Mother Earth.

> *I want to lay down beside you,*
> *And hold your body close to mine.*

Like a grape that grows 'round in the vineyard,
Comes a time we must sip the wine.

Abigail loved that song, even though it annoyed her that *lay* should have been *lie*.

"Proud Mary," Little Willard called the garbage truck. *Help me, Abby,* Little Willard sang in a Brian Wilson falsetto as he nuzzled Abigail's itchy neck, *Help me get her outta my heart.*

And Abigail did help. A baby was conceived that summer on the bench seat of Proud Mary—on July 21, 1969, to be exact—the night that Neil Armstrong walked on the moon. A baby boy was born on April Fools' Day, 1970. The birth of that baby was known to only a few people. Little Willard never knew, nor Goldie, nor Big Willard, and certainly no one in Abigail's family. Thank gawd for distance and lies and excuses and apologies for not going home, even over the holidays, and for '60s fashions like muumuus and caftans and empire-waist peasant dresses that all looked like maternity clothes.

Sherry had a little party for Abigail when she came home from the hospital. There was a sign in Sherry's careful calligraphy just inside the apartment door: THIS IS THE FIRST DAY OF THE REST OF YOUR LIFE. WELCOME HOME, ABBY. Sherry had made a blender full of piña coladas. They drank it all—just the two of them—and made another pitcher and drank that, too, and then they both threw up and went to bed. They never talked about the baby. It was as if Abigail had had an appendectomy.

Abigail graduated from college four weeks later, and when she went home, everyone marveled at how healthy she looked. "Filled out," they said. Abigail went on to graduate school in another state and got a job there, and she never looked back. Only sometimes, that is, like when she saw a baby or a little tow-headed boy who looked like Doc, and every time she put out her garbage, and every April Fools' Day, and whenever someone mentioned the beach, and when the moon was full, and when she saw a photograph of an astronaut, or when a rerun of *Hee-Haw* turned up on the T.V., or a Bugs Bunny cartoon, or a thousand other things. Every day, really, she thought about her baby, imagining him through the years like the pictures of missing children on milk cartons and tucked into utility bills.

But like hundreds of thousands of other women who got pregnant out of wedlock before Roe vs. Wade, Abigail kept it all to herself. Sometimes, though—now that there were so many stories about adopted children finding their birth mothers—when the phone rang, the thought flashed across Abigail's mind when she picked up the receiver that a male voice on the other end of the line might say, "Mother?"

But that call never came.

After an uncomfortable nap on the couch with Richard Burton lying on her legs, Abigail awoke. It was after nine, and she began to wonder if Sissy maybe really was dead. She tiptoed back upstairs. There in her bed, the covers were thrown back, revealing . . . well, we'll skip that.

Abigail gasped and shut the door.

Two hours later, Abigail was fuming mad. She stomped up the stairs and banged on her bedroom door. Sissy came to the door wrapped in Abigail's Laura Ashley aubergine silk comforter, her bony shoulders bare, squirrelly hair disheveled.

"Get dressed, Sissy," Abigail commanded. "This isn't working. Get dressed and I'll drive you home."

Sissy started to protest, but Abigail had had it. She turned and stomped down the stairs, Richard Burton on her heels.

Abigail heard the toilet flush and water run, and Sissy came downstairs, crying.

Abigail would have none of it. She got out her wallet. "Look, Sissy, I'll pay you for your time and for your long walk here, but you have to leave now."

"Oh, please, please, Miss Shapiro," Sissy pleaded. "Please let me stay. I'll clean your house. I don't want no money. Ya don't have to pay me. Please. I'm sorry, Miss Shapiro. I couldn't take no money without doing my work."

"No," Abigail said sternly, trying not to look in Sissy's face.

But then she did look.

And Sissy stayed. She started by cleaning the bathroom, where she took everything out of the medicine cabinet, vanity, and linen closet, put all the jars and bottles in the bathtub, filled the tub with water, and scrubbed the containers. She moved on to Abigail's bedroom, where she emptied her closet and drawers and tried on her clothes.

Abigail was exasperated. She served tomato sandwiches for lunch, and Sissy ate silently, not asking for seconds. By 5:00 p.m., Abigail had had enough, although Sissy was still "working." Oh, she did dust and she did vacuum and she did scrub, but Abigail wanted her gone.

"Listen, Sissy," Abigail said, after Sissy had taken all of Abigail's CDs out of their cases and put them in the dishwasher, "I have to go out now. What do you say we call it a day? You've done a fine job. I'll pay you and drive you home." She opened her wallet and handed Sissy three twenty dollar bills.

"Okay," Sissy agreed, and Abigail sighed.

In the car, Abigail started down Grand Street, toward downtown and Route 119 North. "Osage, right?" Abigail asked.

"Well," Sissy said and paused. "I don't live there no more. Could ya drive me to my boyfriend's house?"

Okay. Anywhere, Abigail thought. *ANY. WHERE.* "Where does your boyfriend live?"

"Weston," Sissy answered.

Weston was seventy miles away, three towns down I-79 South.

"Weston?"

Sissy nodded.

They had driven in silence for nearly fifty minutes when Sissy asked, "Is Weston this far?"

"Well, yes," Abigail answered. "It's about ten more miles. Weston is where your boyfriend lives, is it not?"

"I'm not sure," Sissy whispered.

"What the hell do you mean?" Abigail shouted, having lost her patience. "For chrissake, does he live in Weston, or doesn't he?" Sissy started to cry. Abigail made a U-turn across the median and headed back toward Morgantown. By this time, it had begun to pour.

"Sissy, how can you not know where he lives?" Abigail asked irritably as she strained to see through the sheet of rain.

"Well, he doesn't live nowhere, really," Sissy answered.

"What do you mean, 'he doesn't live nowhere really?'"

"Well, he's a soy-joiner."

"A *what?*" Abigail imagined someone fashioning dove-tailed joints out of tofu.

"A soy-joiner."

"Soy-joiner?"

"Ya know, soy-joiner, someone who travels. Professionally. From place to place." She pronounced 'professionally' with the accent on the first syllable.

"A journeyman?"

"No, a soy-joiner."

A few miles later, it dawned on Abigail what Sissy was saying: *sojourner.* A professional sojourner?

"Sissy, what does your boyfriend do for a living? Where does he work?"

"He's a prophet . . . a preacher," Sissy said proudly, sitting up tall.

"What's his name?"

"Zero."

"Zero? What's his last name?"

"Prophet Zero."

"Prophet Zero?" Abigail asked. "Well, where does this Prophet Zero preach? Does he have a church?"

"He's not from around here," Sissy answered. "Zero's church is the universe, he says. He's a street preacher." She pronounced 'universe' 'you-knee-verse'. She paused. "He preachers out front of Family Dollar."

How could Abigail not have seen the woman driving the 29-ft Winnebago, a Norwegian elkhound riding shotgun, coming up in the passing lane beside her? Well, the wind was blowing, and the rain was coming down in sheets, blasting them like they were trapped in a high-speed automatic car wash. Abigail came over a rise and swerved into the passing lane to avoid a dead deer—half on the shoulder, half in her lane—and BAM! The impact sent her little PT Cruiser spinning. The last sound she heard before the air bag exploded was Sissy's scream. And then more spinning and another loud smack and the tinkling of glass, muffled by the punch of the airbag. Abigail was shaken but basically unharmed. The passenger airbag, however, had failed to inflate, and Sissy's right forearm, shoulder, and thumb were smashed against the door when the PT Cruiser slid into an embankment and came to a stop. The car was totaled, and Sissy was extracted from the vehicle with the Jaws of Life.

It was almost midnight when they left the emergency room, Sissy with a cast from her shoulder to her hand.

Thank God for the doggie door, Abigail thought as the taxi dropped them off in front of her house. Poor Richard Burton had been home alone for over seven hours. He was frantic to see her and came running to the door, smiling and squeaking his rubber hamburger, jumping in the air and spinning about like a boxing kangaroo.

In the kitchen, Abigail fixed Richard Burton his dinner, took out two wine glasses, opened a bottle of Malbec, and poured a glass for herself and one for Sissy.

"I don't drink, Miss Shapiro," Sissy protested.

"You do now," Abigail said, sipping her wine. "To life," Abigail said, clinking Sissy's glass.

"To the Jaws of Life!" Sissy added.

Sissy smiled weakly then guzzled her glass of wine in one gulp.

What else could Abigail have done but bring Sissy to her house? Have the taxi drop her off in front of Family Dollar at midnight? She felt responsible for Sissy now. Sissy and her cast.

"I'm so sorry, Sissy," Abigail said and started to cry. Richard Burton jumped up on her lap to protect her from whatever it was that was making her cry.

"Oh, Miss Shapiro, it's all my fault. I'm sorry, too," Sissy said, wiping her eyes with the back of her cast-free hand and sniffling.

"No, Sissy, it's my fault. I didn't see that Winnebago."

"Ya couldn't, Miss Shapiro. Ya couldn't see through the rain. If it weren't for me, we wouldn't have been out on that there inner state anyways," and she started to bawl.

Abigail poured herself and Sissy another glass of wine.

"I don't know what's the matter with me," Sissy cried. "Everything

I touch turns to shit. It's just me. It's in my blood. It's all my peoples. Nothing good ever happens to any of us. Only the bad come knockin'."

The way Sissy said "my peoples" made Abigail's heart hurt. It was a country way of talking, a way of saying not just family, but the whole lot, generation after generation, past and future hopeless, end-less, doomed.

And then Sissy opened up to Abigail, releasing a whole flood of heartaches. She'd had five children, she told Abigail. Wick, the old-est had been stabbed to death in a bar fight downtown, outside Club Z, three years ago. And Dawson, her second oldest, was in prison for dealing crystal meth. Azalea, her daughter, had "run off" when she was fifteen, and two others—Timmy Dal and Rose—had died as infants. "Crib deaths," Sissy said, and started to cry harder. "But I ain't sure. I was working both times, and when I come home they was dead. I sometimes think Dal—" Dal, Abigail supposed, was the no-good dead husband. She didn't want to think about what he might have done.

And then for some reason, Abigail told her. She told Sissy about Little Willard and the baby, something she'd never told anyone all these years. She couldn't believe she was saying it. It was something she'd kept inside her like a stone. Something all buried and mossed over. She'd never even told Frank McDonough, even after they went to couples counseling, and he admitted that one summer he'd spent in Europe he'd had an affair with a man. He wasn't gay, he insisted, nor even bisexual; he was young, and it just happened. He was seduced by the older man's élan and he'd been ashamed ever since. He never told anyone. Anyone. But he wanted to be honest with Abigail like the counselor said they should be—"pull out all the plugs." And after talking about that indiscretion, he felt better, "like a great weight had been lifted," he said. Barbie Maynard, the counselor, helped Frank see that the older man was a sexual predator and had probably lured other young college boys the same way, under the false pretense of help, gen-erosity, and friendship, and that that one sexual adventure didn't mean that Frank was gay. (Frank, however, failed to mention that whenever he and Abigail had sex he wanted her to stick a carrot up his butt.)

Frank wanted Abigail to know everything about him, he said. He didn't want any secrets between them. He wanted their relationship to work out. He wanted to marry her. The whole counseling session was an opportunity for Abigail to open up, too. "Touching the pain," Barbie Maynard called it. But Abigail didn't open up. She kept her mouth shut. She didn't touch anything.

Why did some people think they had to know everything . . . and that everybody else needed to know it, too? What was wrong with mystery? And privacy? Why did some people have to drag everything out of their closets and attics and basements and garages and display it all on the lawn with a price tag? And some of them went so far as to write about it all . . . and publish it!

"Oh, Miss Shapiro," Sissy said after Abigail told her, "You is better off without that baby. Children only break your heart. They break it every day for as long as ya live. Even after they's dead and gone. And that's the Lord's truth. As long as ya live."

Abigail knew Sissy was right. She'd seen it happen again and again. Children dying and children strung out on drugs. Children in prison and children estranged. Sociopathic children and children with children. Children breaking their parents' hearts, bankrupting them, and ruining their lives. And that was just the ones you knew. What about all the people in the world who acted normal but had their own secret torments that nobody—least of all their parents—knew anything about?

And then there was that story a few years ago about the young man who showed up on someone's doorstep, claiming to be an illegitimate son, demanding a substantial chunk of money. That young man totally destroyed that family. The wife divorced her husband, and then the husband ended up killing himself, and in the end the guy wasn't a son at all. It was all a scam. Well, at least if you were a woman you knew for damn sure how many children you'd had. Maybe Abigail should get an unlisted phone number. Maybe even change her name.

Yes, it was just like Sissy said. Children will break your heart. What a risk it was to procreate. If anybody really thought about it, they would never do it. They'd get a dog instead. At least a bad dog you could have put down. And probably, the parents with kids who turned out even halfway decent didn't really appreciate their good fortune or the terrible risk they'd taken. And for those whose children went amiss, well . . . God bless all of them.

But why did people do it? Why did they keep procreating? The world was a mess: senseless wars and acts of terrorism; irreparable environmental degradation; nuclear disasters, nuclear threats; contaminated food supplies, dioxin in the water, heavy metals in the air; economic mayhem; corruption, greed, poverty, brutality, drugs. You name it. And natural disasters one after another. Earthquakes to the left of them! Tsunamis to the right! Had Mother Nature had it up to her ears with humankind, too? Every time Abigail saw a headline or heard a news report, an image came to her, a picture of herself sitting on the plaid couch in Goldie and Big Willard's trailer, Little Willard's arm around her, Buck Owens and Roy Clark singing "Gloom, Despair, and Agony on Me," all of them—even little Doc—singing along. And where, she wondered, where were they now—Goldie and all the Willards?

And just yesterday she'd received an invitation to a baby shower. It was for Sylvia Phillips, someone she barely knew. This was the Phillips's sixth, maybe seventh or even eighth child! Who could keep track? For crying out loud! Consumers, all of them. Who did the Phillipses think they were? Abigail wanted to write STOP IT! on the R.S.V.P. card and send it back, but she just threw the damn thing away. Truth was, reproduction just didn't interest her.

And then there was that other guy she'd worked with—Gary something—who also had six or seven or eight kids and said gaily that they'd just keep having them until God told them to stop. You know what I'd say if I was his wife? Abigail thought when he said that: *"Gary, I heard a voice last night. You were asleep . . ."*

But people did, they did want babies. Think of old Antoinetta Cassuccio down the street, who was in her nineties and visited the cemetery every day where she'd buried five infants. And Tolstoy: he'd buried five children . . . and fathered seven more!

Children, Abigail concluded, like gardens and diets, were an expression of hope and optimism. Abigail herself was overweight and loathed gardening.

Truth was, Abigail admitted to herself, she had never wanted that baby. If she had, she would have kept it. What had stopped her? What stopped her was that she didn't have one maternal bone in her whole body; all she had was guilt, guilt for the way she was, the way she felt. And one reason she never told anybody about the baby was because she didn't want to admit to being a link in Goldie and Big Willard's chain of being. She was ashamed of them, too. But now, when she thought about them and Little Willard, about sitting with them in their trailer, eating Cheetos and Vienna sausages, and drinking Riunite out of plastic *Happy Days* cups, she realized they were some of the nicest people she'd ever known. They weren't pretentious and cutthroat, greedy and ambitious, self-important and puffed up, like half the people she knew now. Salt of the earth, is what Goldie and Big Willard were. They were the same noble stock, weren't they, as the Ricketts and the Woodses and the Gudgers—the people James Agee had written about in *Let Us Now Praise Famous Men*? And they were nonjudgmental. They would have accepted her into the family with open arms. Welcomed her. Still, it wasn't the life she wanted. She wanted something better than a garbage truck in the front yard.

What kind of monster was she? Abigail thought about all the sock monkeys she'd grudgingly made, all the babies she'd pretended to adore. They elicited no real love. Nor envy. Nothing ever tasted as good as that first piña colada and first cigarette after the birth of her baby, after all those months of abstinence.

Oh, Abigail Shapiro was a bitter, heartless bitch. *Heart like a stone,* some would say. And she was selfish, too. She knew that. She would have made a terrible mother.

But she loved Richard Burton. She loved her dog. That was certain. No one could ever say that Abigail Shapiro wasn't a good dog mother.

She felt better after telling Sissy, admitting the truth. It was like a great weight had been lifted—like Frank McDonough had said after his big, blurting confession.

Good gawd, Abigail was drunk. The wine bottle was empty, and Abigail opened another, but before they'd finished it, Sissy put her head down again on the table.

"Sissy," Abigail coaxed, "come on, Sissy. Come to bed. I'll help you. Come to bed."

Abigail led Sissy upstairs, and while Sissy was in the bathroom, Abigail pulled out a pair of her nicest, freshly laundered Laura Ashley pajamas and opened the bathroom door a crack and handed them to Sissy.

Recently, Abigail had purchased a dozen greeting cards that were cutouts of Munch's *The Scream*, blank inside. It was a good reproduction, and the cards stood up like paper dolls. More and more, it seemed to her that *The Scream* card was appropriate for all occasions: birth, birthday, graduation, wedding, anniversary, new job, new home, retirement, sympathy, get well . . . anything, really. As she was retrieving the pajamas from a bureau drawer, she noticed that Sissy had taken all twelve cards and lined them up as if they were marching across the bureau top against the mirror. They looked nice there, too, Abigail had to hand it to Sissy on that count.

Back in the bedroom, Abigail pulled down the covers, and Sissy climbed in.

There wasn't another bed in the house since Abigail had converted one of the three bedrooms into her study and the other to expand the bathroom and build a dressing room and walk-in closet. She never had any overnight company any more—she didn't want any—and the fact that she had only one bed sent a message loud and clear that overnight guests were not welcome.

She would sleep on the couch.

She tucked Sissy in, but then, suddenly, overcome with exhaustion and wine, she climbed in beside her. Richard Burton jumped up between them, digging in the pillows and grunting before he settled in.

"Good night, Mish Shapiro," Sissy said, her speech a little slurred.

"Abby," Abigail said. "Please, Sissy, no more Miss Shapiro. Just call me Abby."

"Abby," Sissy whispered, "that's a right purty name. It fits ya." No sooner had she spoken than she was fast asleep.

A dog down the street began to bark—it sounded like Henrietta, the poor, sweet, friendly Goldendoodle who was always chained outside—and then another and another. Someone must be walking down the alley, Abigail thought. Richard Burton, always eager to join in a barking match, slept through the ruckus. His ears twitched. He licked his lips and sighed. Abigail glanced at the clock—nearly three—and turned off her Laura Ashley ginger jar lamp.

✦ Help Wanted: Female ✦

PART I

HELP WANTED: WORD PROCESSOR. BG&D, INC. CALL 344-662-9000 TO MAKE AN APPOINTMENT FOR AN INTERVIEW SCREENING AND SECURITY CLEARANCE.

Word PROCESSOR? *What could that mean?* Wendy wondered out loud, circling the help-wanted ad with a Maybelline eyebrow pencil.

One who processes *words?* To process *words?*

She reached for her *American Heritage Dictionary.*

PROCESS: 1. a progression. (*Of words?*) 2. the act of proceeding or coming forth. (*Of words?*) 3. a marching. (*Of words?*)

Wendy had been out of work for almost two months. Her rent was due. Again. And she wasn't eligible for unemployment because she'd not been laid off; she'd quit. Many jobs, in fact. Her most recent job as a furniture repossessor for Cohen Furniture had lasted only one-half day. And before that, her job as the assistant to a private investigator had lasted only two. In that job, Wendy was supposed to drive to a low-life bar called the Rainbow, way out on the Grafton Road, and chat up a guy named Harlan Doyle, a voice-activated tape recorder the size of a box of Chiclets concealed in her pocket. In the wallet-size photo Wendy had been given by J. Gamble, P.I., Harlan Doyle sported an upper-lip-obscuring Tom Selleck moustache; a shiny, deep-V shirt that showcased a gold chain nestling in the pelt of his chest fur; and a mullet so extreme that Wendy at first mistook it for a coonskin cap.

J. Gamble, P.I., had been hired by Cheryl Doyle, the philanderer's similarly mulleted wife, who stood behind Harlan in the Olan Mills portrait, her right hand—missing its index finger—clamped onto Harlan's shoulder like a bald eagle's talon.

Wendy drove out to The Rainbow, her Irish wolfhound, William Butler Yeats, fidgeting about in the backseat of her Plymouth Horizon like a horse trying to make itself comfortable on a loveseat. The Rainbow's parking lot was mud, crowded with pickups, and dark as Hades. The "R," the "i," and the "w" in the neon sign were burned out, as well as all the colors of the rainbow above it, except yellow. "_a_nbo_" the sign said, with half a McDonald-esque golden arch dangling above it. Similarly challenged beer advertisements in the filthy, blackened windows offered "S_h_itz" and "_ud___ser" beer.

Wendy sat in her car, listening to the Talking Heads. "I don't know about this, Bill," she said to her dog and then drove back home.

There had to be a better job out there. Somewhere.

BG&D was a contractor to the government—the Department of Energy complex out on the Collins Ferry Road. The BG&D word-processing center was a cement hive, a large, windowless, basement room with a drop ceiling and jitterbuzzing fluorescent lights, a cinderblock building in the wayback of the compound, next to the containment pond for slurry from an experimental coal-fired power plant, which loomed over the hive. Grendel, Wendy called the power plant. Every Monday morning, a guy in a white Tyvek space suit, complete with padded gloves, space boots, and diving-bell-type helmet, stepped out of a Haz-Mat van, waddled up to the pond, dipped a test tube in the water, waddled back to the van holding the test tube at arm's length like a dirty diaper, and drove away. Throughout the day, whitetail deer grazed on the bright green grass surrounding the pond and quenched their thirst at the bright blue water's edge.

By some miracle, Wendy was hired as a word processor at BG&D, in spite of the fact that she had no experience and no references. Word processing, she learned, was glorified typing—a mix of typesetting and just plain old typing—using a mainframe computer. And Wendy landed the job because she could type. Boy, could she type. She was an excellent typist.

In high school, she'd been part of an experimental typing class. Students used the standard electric typewriters with unmarked keys and a map of the keyboard on a pull-down blind in the front of the room, which remained pulled down for only the first couple of weeks. But the experimental part was this: they typed to music. They started out with "The Syncopated Clock" and progressed through "Surrey with the Fringe on Top" and "The Daring Young Man on the Flying Trapeze," and by the end of the semester, they were typing to "Flight of the Bumblebee."

The secret was to find the rhythm in the syntax and keep a song in your head while you typed. Easy. There were always songs in Wendy's head. Her typing teacher, Miss Minnick, was a genius. It was from Miss Minnick that Wendy learned how all of Emily Dickinson's poems can be typed—and sung—to "The Yellow Rose of Texas."

> *I heard a fly buzz when I died;*
> *The stillness round my form*
> *Was like the stillness in the air*
> *Between the heaves of storm.*

Along with Wendy, three other future word processors were hired to join BG&D that fall of 1985. One was a young black guy named Roger, who could type even faster and more accurately than Wendy. Everyone else in the word processing pool was female, all of them young and single, most of them divorced, many with small children.

"I *love* your earrings," Roger leaned over and whispered to Wendy during their first training session. One of Wendy's earrings was a pink plastic ringer washing machine about the size of a shot glass; its mate, a turquoise dryer. "Where did you get them?"

"At that junkie kiosk in the old mall," Wendy replied, "Jewelry-R-Us—or something like that."

"Do you think they have any more?" Roger wanted to know.

Wendy sensed a kindred spirit. "Let's go check it out after work," she suggested.

Instantly, Roger and Wendy were best friends. On Saturdays, they combed the yard sales and flea markets and Volunteers of Americas, the Goodwills and the Salvation Armies, searching for discarded treasures. On Saturday nights, Wendy and Roger went to the transvestite bar downtown, Vice Versa. In her garage apartment, clad in Wendy's faux leopard-skin bikini and her stepmother's cast-off mink, Roger rehearsed his Vice Versa skit, working up his courage to do his karaoke impersonation of Eartha Kitt singing, *Mink Shmink, Money Shmoney* . . .

It was in word processing training at BG&D that Wendy first learned about cut and paste. She had an IBM Selectric typewriter—her prized possession—which she thought was the cat's pajamas because it had two interchangeable font balls: one courier, one script. She used to try to write poetry, but the problem was this: as soon as she rolled her poem off the platen, she wanted to change a word or a line—or even a whole stanza, which involved either retyping the entire poem or a word or a line, cutting it out carefully with scissors, spraying the back with hair spray, and then *very* carefully—with tweezers—placing it over the egregious text and then taping over it, or cutting out entire stanzas, rearranging them, and taping them on a blank piece of paper. Without a light box or waxer.

When Wendy saw the demonstration of cut and paste in the BG&D word processing training, she felt like Blake seeing God. She jumped out of her chair and screamed, "Oh my gawd! Oh my gawd! Holy shit! You can cut and paste! You. Can. Cut. And. You. Can. Paste! OH MY GAWD! CUT AND PASTE!"

Everyone stared at her like she was from another planet.

"Curb your enthusiasm," Roger said dryly, tugging on Wendy's skirt, the one with the bowling pins and bowling balls silk-screened on it, and Wendy sat down.

"Roger," Wendy leaned over and whispered to him, "but Roger, don't you see? This is the great invention of our time."

"Not," Roger whispered back, still typing a mile a minute. "Spandex is the great invention of our time; you know that as well as I."

The director of the BG&D word processing center was a fiftysomething ex-military guy named Bob Boldt, who looked like Anthony Hopkins. He was a creep from the word go. Little Big Man, Roger and Wendy called him, or just LBM. In the back of the word processing center was a glass mezzanine with a wall of windows, which was Little Big Man's office—an observatory from where he could watch the word processing staff as they all faced forward, processing words.

Wendy didn't like the fact that day after day, week after week, someone was looking down on her, watching her process words, so one day she brought a make-up mirror in and placed it on her work station, tilted up at LBM's office windows.

The mirror lasted about fifteen minutes before it was confiscated by Pamela, the lead operator and right hand of Little Big Man.

"Against regulations," Pamela pronounced, making a show of dropping Wendy's mirror with a crash and tinkle into the regulation government-issue gray-green metal trash can.

Every few days, someone was called into Little Big Man's office, and the Venetian blinds were closed. The summons was delivered by Pamela. A tap on the shoulder, hushed directives.

Roger and Wendy would look at each other and make *The Scream* face. Would one of them be next? Was it a reprimand or something more sinister? Roger speculated that the office of *le Petit Grand Homme* (as he sometimes called LBM) was a torture chamber, outfitted with hooks and whips.

Every woman tapped returned ashen, mum.

The day after the purloined mirror, Wendy was tapped.

"Come in! Come in," Little Big Man said in an overzealous welcome, his hand lightly touching the small of Wendy's back. "And welcome. Welcome to BG&D."

Wendy cringed.

"I like to get to know all my girls personally," Little Big Man said, "and I want you to know me. We're a family," he said. "Just think of me as Uncle Bob," he chuckled. And then with his hand on Wendy's shoulder, he whispered close to her ear, "but don't tell any of the higher-ups I said that." (Chuckle. Chuckle.)

"Lord have mercy upon us. Christ have mercy upon us," Wendy chanted to herself. "Gag me with a spoon."

"Sit down. Sit down," Little Big Man said, motioning toward a low chair in front of his desk. "It's so nice to have you join us, Wendy. You're an excellent typist I hear, and a college graduate, too! Well, good for you! Good for you! A degree in *English*! Good for you! And just what *is* a degree in English?"

By this time, Little Big Man had sat down on his big desk right in front of Wendy, his crotch in her face.

"Uhmmm," Wendy replied, looking at the ceiling. "I—uh, I—uh— I read a lot of books," she said quickly.

"Really?" he said, "Well, good for you! Good for you! What kind of books?"

"Literature," Wendy said.

"Literature! Well now, isn't that something? Good for you! I'm not much of a reader myself," Little Big Man continued. "I'm an action man. I play tennis and handball, and of course, I golf, and I work out every day, and I swim. I have a boat. I have a beautiful 1979 Chris-Craft 350 Catalina cabin cruiser out on Cheat Lake. Do you like to swim, Wendy?"

"No," Wendy said. "I'm a sinker."

"A sinker! Oh, come on now!"

"No, really, I hate water. I hate boats."

"Oh, no, nobody hates water! I could teach you how to swim, Wendy. You'd love it. Why don't you let me teach you how to swim, Wendy?"

"Listen, Mr. Boldt," Wendy said, "I really have to get back to work. I'm working on something for Mr. Manillo that's very important. High priority." She started to get up.

"Oh, don't run off, Wendy," Little Big Man said, leaning forward and blocking her exit from the low chair. "It can wait. Mr. Manillo's not in charge here. I am."

"No, really," Wendy said, jumping up and pushing past him. "It's been very nice talking to you," she said, heading out the door.

Wendy ran to the ladies' room, shaking, and splashed cold water on her face.

She wished she had a cigarette.

"You look like Death eating a cracker," Roger said to her when she returned to her chair. "What was it like up there?"

Wendy couldn't speak.

"He's a perv, isn't he?" Roger said. "He is! I knew it! I knew it! Oh, I wish he'd call me up there. I *live* for the day when Pamela taps me. I'll show him a thing or two."

Back in 1967, when Wendy was in high school and looking for her first part-time job, classified job advertisements said HELP WANTED: MALE, HELP WANTED: FEMALE, HELP WANTED: MALE OR FEMALE. The male help-wanted jobs always required brawn and what were considered strictly male skills like the ability to operate machinery without getting your hair caught in it, a threatening enough presence to work alone at night, and low-level thinking and decision-making skills: gas station attendant, construction or maintenance worker, delivery man, truck driver, night watchman, custodian, liquor store clerk.

The female jobs were all about typing and organizing things and filing papers and greeting customers and cleaning and being polite and friendly and helpful, and changing diapers and caring for people, especially children, invalids, and the elderly. Jobs like typist, secretary, receptionist, file clerk, housekeeper, maid, babysitter, home companion, telephone operator, sales clerk—Domestics.

HELP WANTED: MALE OR FEMALE jobs were possibly something a woman could do, but a man was clearly preferred, and a woman would be hired only as a last resort—something usually in a restaurant like short-order cook or dishwasher, or something that involved machinery or tools other than a typewriter or vacuum cleaner.

Although the sexist headings had been removed from the job advertisements by the '80s, the discrimination remained, and sometimes Wendy felt that even her college degree was held against her—she was "overeducated" for the job, one interviewer told her. Wendy's bachelor's degree in English was basically useless, unless she wanted to teach, but all the English teaching jobs were taken. "Did you get fries with that?" was the standard joke about a degree in English.

Wendy was so upset by her encounter with Little Big Man that she never wanted to go back to the word processing pool. But, of course, she was flat broke. According to her calculations, which were always wrong and always in her favor, she had $13 in her checking account. And no savings whatsoever. She needed the job, even if it paid only minimum wage. Back then, she didn't know how to be assertive. Her only response to anger was passive aggressiveness. She didn't know shit about sexual harassment, either. She didn't even know how to pronounce it correctly.

So she responded in the only way she knew how.

The next day, Wendy wore a man's suit to work. Her vintage shark-skin. Underneath it, she wore her Day-Glo green t-shirt and a big wide bright yellow tie with an eye chart on it. She tore off a piece of Saran wrap about six-feet long and tied it around her head in a big bow. She wore her Chuck Taylor hightops and pinned a big black metal button the size of a gas cap on her lapel. In bold white Helvetica, the button said, THERE'S THAT SMELL AGAIN.

She wore the same outfit four days in a row.

And then she was tapped.

"Wendy!" Little Big Man said, "Come in. Come in. Sit down! Sit down!"

"I prefer not," Wendy said. Standing, Wendy was at least two inches taller than Little Big Man.

"Oh, no, sit down, sit down," he said, motioning toward the low chair.

"No," she said. "No thank you."

"Sit down," LBM commanded. His neck was so red it looked like a gigantic strawberry Twizzler.

"No," Wendy said.

"And what's this?" he said, tap-tap-tap-tapping the button on Wendy's lapel with his index finger. "What smell?"

Wendy was shaking. "I don't know," she said.

"You don't know! Well, surely you know! You're wearing that button. So, what's that smell? Is it *me*? Is it *me* that you smell, Wendy? Do I smell good, Wendy? Do you want to smell me, Wendy, is that it?"

Wendy couldn't speak.

"Take that button off right now," LBM said. "Take it off right now, and hand it to me."

Wendy couldn't move.

"Take it off, or I'll take it off for you."

"Don't you dare touch me," Wendy said.

"Don't touch me!" Little Big Man said in a high squeaky voice. He looked like he was about to explode. "Don't touch me. Don't touch me. I have a degree in *English*. I've read a lot of books."

As Wendy turned to leave, Little Big Man grabbed her arm. "Listen to me, you little cunt. Get out of here. Off the premises. And when you come back, you better not be wearing that fuckin' cunt-ass button. And the next time I see you, you better be dressed like a woman."

Wendy ran out. Back to Word Processing. She grabbed her purse and left. Roger came running down the hall after her.

"Go back! Go back!" Wendy said. "Bad dog. Stay."

Wendy went home and got in bed. William Butler Yeats plopped down on the floor beside her and rested his chin on the bed, which was really an army cot.

Wendy had always had a penchant for vintage clothes and costumes and had accumulated an eclectic, eccentric wardrobe. Along one wall of her garage apartment, she'd erected a clothesline, which sagged under the weight of hangers bearing vintage dresses and mouton, raccoon, and Persian lamb coats. The opposite wall was covered with hats of all shapes and sizes, and beneath them, shelves made of boards and bricks were stacked with shoes. An old Hoosier cabinet was home to 1950s beaded sweaters, satin bed jackets, wigs, ties, a shoe box of rhinestone pins and slogan buttons, etc. All of it had come her way for pennies from flea markets, yard sales, junk stores, Goodwills, Volunteers of Americas, and church bazaars.

Her love of costumes had started when she was a little girl. Wendy's parents had been in the theater, and there was a big hump-backed tin trunk in their attic, full of gowns and costumes and accessories. Before she started school, Wendy often got up in the morning, put on a costume, and wore it all day. Sometimes she was Hans Brinker, the little Dutch boy, like on the cans of paint stacked in the garage. The little Dutch boy wore voluminous blue bloomers and a muffin hat, and clomped around in a big pair of wooden shoes. Sometimes she was Little Mary Sunshine in a long yellow lace dress and a tattered picture hat, or Annie Oakley, or Pocahontas, or Abe Lincoln with a long moth-eaten beard and a shredded silk stovepipe hat waiting for a snowman to happen. There was even a horse costume, meant to be worn by two people, but sometimes Wendy just wore the head or carried it around like a teddy bear. Wendy's mother called her "The Headless Horseman's Headless Horsehead."

Wendy's problem with authority may have started the day her mother let her wear a pirate costume on her first day of school. Wendy loved the pirate costume. It was from the Gilbert and Sullivan light opera *The Pirates of Penzance* and had striped pantaloons, a big red sash, a black felt vest with gold braid, a headkerchief, and an eye patch. On her first day of school, Wendy ran around the classroom with a rubber knife clenched between her teeth, brandishing a cardboard sword.

Until the principal escorted her into the hall. To Wendy's sister's great embarrassment, Mr. McLaughlin then removed *her* from her third-grade classroom and instructed her to walk Pirate Wendy home, bearing a note for their mother. From then on, Wendy reluctantly wore the requisite plaid puff-sleeve dresses with sashes and sometimes an organdy pinafore.

But whenever there was an opportunity to wear a costume or uniform or something weird, Wendy jumped at the chance. Even in a hat or wig, she felt empowered. Like she was somebody other than Wendy. She insisted on taking ballet lessons—even though she had two flat left feet—just for the tutu and pink tights, the leotard and ballet slippers. She played softball just for the uniform, the cap, and the mitt, even though her nickname was Easy Out, and on the rare occasion when far out in right field the ball came her way, Wendy ducked.

She couldn't wait to be a Brownie. She begged and begged until she got the whole shebang: the Brownie uniform, the Brownie beanie, the Brownie pin, scarf, handkerchief, and socks, and even the Buster Brown Brownie shoes. But she only lasted a month or so in her Brownie troop—until Halloween rolled around and she refused to bob for apples.

The Brownie leader, tough old Miss Witherspoon, stuck Wendy's head in the washtub of water and apples and held it there until she almost drowned. Wendy kicked her in the shin with her sturdy Buster Brown Brownie shoes and ran home. She never went back (although she continued to wear the Brownie uniform to school every Tuesday, much to the real Brownies' dismay).

It was a Friday in mid-October when Little Big Man told Wendy to go home and change her clothes. That weekend, she and Roger went to check out a new store that had popped up in one of the vacant storefronts in the old mall, which had been taken over by senior citizens who arrived in their Senior Monongalians bus and traversed the mall's corridors in their Nikes for cardiovascular well-being while the bus driver sat on one of the mall's benches, chain smoking. The two anchor stores—Montgomery Wards and Sears—had long ago jumped ship, and little by little the other stores—Hallmark Cards, Radio Shack, Florsheim Shoes, Olan Mills Studios, Kuehn Jewelers, the pet store, the Pretzel Palace—left, too, and all that remained was Goodwill Industries, Family Dollar, and the 24-Hour No. 2 Happy All-You-Can-Eat Chinese Buffet, which attracted some of the largest humans ever to roam the earth.

At the new store—the Little Shop of Horrors—Wendy was immediately drawn to the gorilla costume. It cost $40 to rent for three days. She knew she couldn't afford it; it was more than half her weekly paycheck, and she had necessities to buy: cigarettes, toilet paper, Tampax, dog food, ramen noodles. Still, she wanted the gorilla costume. She wanted a disguise, something she could don and run around in, pounding her chest and screaming. Even though on the outside, she looked like a timid, 110-lb., thirtysomething woman, inside Wendy was a raging King Kong.

Wendy was sick and mad and depressed and angry. She was angry at her husband for leaving her for a woman who was way younger, way prettier, way taller, way sexier, way more accomplished, way more sophisticated, and way wealthier than she. The woman's name was Georgie di Giorgio, and she was an architect, a partner in her father's architectural firm. Her father was a multimillionaire who had hired Wendy's husband to build him a mansion—a house that Georgie designed—meant to look like the prow of a glass ship rising above the dunes on the Outer Banks where the di Giorgios vacationed.

One night during dinner, Wendy's husband told her that Georgie had told him that she'd known she wanted to be an architect ever since she was a toddler. Her earliest memory was of being three years old and building the Seven Wonders of the Ancient World out of Legos—totally by herself, of course, and without instructions—only to be "supremely disappointed" in their size. She needed to work with big things, she said. The bigger the better. (Wendy's earliest recollection was of eating the lead paint off of her crib.) The disclosure about Georgie's earliest memory escalated to a screaming match between Wendy and her husband after Wendy made some snide remark about Georgie's big ass. "You're so fuckin' stupid," Wendy's husband screamed at her while sweeping his plate of Hamburger Helper to the floor, "you don't even know the difference between soffit and fascia."

Georgie di Giorgio had legs up to Wendy's armpits and good bone structure and Etienne Aigner boots, and she drove a Beemer. Wendy hated her and her privileged background. She hated her for stealing her husband, even though she hated him, too. More even. When he came to the beach to check on the progress of his glass house, Georgie di Giorgio's father ate breakfast every morning in the restaurant where Wendy worked before she left town. He routinely left $20 tips for breakfast, and once Wendy tore up one of his $20 bills right in the middle of the dining room, and another time, she set one of his $20 tips on fire.

Wendy was angry and depressed because her parents were dead. She was angry and depressed because her friend Lynn had been killed by a drunk driver earlier that year. She was angry and depressed because the weekend Lynn was killed, Wendy was taking care of Lynn's dog, an Irish wolfhound named William Butler Yeats, and now, somehow, William Butler Yeats was Wendy's dog. And she was allergic to him. She lived in a one-car garage converted into an apartment. It was like an aluminum storage shed with a kitchen area and small bathroom and four small windows in the garage door, and she wasn't supposed to have pets. How long can you hide a one-hundred-forty-pound Irish wolfhound in a two-hundred-square-foot living space? William Butler Yeats was bigger than Wendy and ate way more. He was so tall that he could look out the tiny windows at the top of the garage door while standing on all fours. Someone was bound to see him looking out and report him to Wendy's landlord, Jasper Quince.

Wendy was angry, too, about all the jobs she'd had where workers were treated like shit. Angry at employers like BG&D where female employees were "required to volunteer" to work for free on Saturdays, serving drinks to male DOE employees at tailgating parties prior to West Virginia University home football games. Angry at men (except Roger). Angry about all the inequality in the world, about all the women (and Roger) in the word processing pool at BG&D, who, like herself, were working 39.5 hours a week for minimum wage, without benefits. Every Friday, the entire word processing pool was dismissed from work a half hour early, and that half-hour release disqualified them from benefits.

Roger, the voice of reason, persuaded Wendy not to rent the gorilla costume. "Listen," he said, "you step out of your car at BG&D dressed like a gorilla, and they'll fuckin' shoot you. They'll shoot you dead. BAM! And that will be that."

Wendy knew Roger was right, but still, the gorilla costume called to her. *"Wen-deeeee,"* it whispered. *"Wen-deeeeeee!"*

"Why not this?" Roger said, holding up a white rabbit costume, which cost only $12 for a one-week rental. It was white fleece with a zipper up the front and a hood and an enormous fluffy pom-pom for a tail. It had white mittens with pink velveteen palms and white slippers with pink rubber soles to wear over your shoes, and big, white, bendable ears with pink velveteen lining. All Wendy would need, Roger pointed out, was whiskers and a pink nose.

"You know . . ." Roger said, slipping into his Gracie Slick routine, *One pill makes you larger, and one pill makes you small . . .*

Sunday night, Wendy dreamed a lucid dream. She was sitting in her appointed chair in the Word Processing center, next to Roger, typing away, and her chair started to wiggle. It wobbled and wiggled. Wendy thought she was imagining the movement. But then the chair started to tilt and levitate and whirl. And before she knew it, the slight levitation took on

Mary Poppins' proportions, and Wendy was up near the ceiling, holding on to the sides of her chair, giggling. And then the ceiling opened up like a box top. The stars where twinkling, and all the BG&D word processors and Little Big Man were looking up at her, their faces small as dimes. The slurry containment pond shimmered, and the whitetail deer danced around it on their hind legs, like children playing Ring Around the Rosy. She saw the Milky Way like a big cosmic scuff mark on dark blue linoleum. There were comets and shooting stars and all kinds of flashing, swirling colors like a psychedelic light show. The man in the moon winked at her and told her to throw away her *GPO Style Manual*. She saw the whole Department of Energy complex spread out beneath her like a tablecloth. *"Thou preparest a table before me in the presence of mine enemies,"* she said to herself. Up and up she ascended, like Remedios the Beauty. Wendy felt so happy and free, and just like in a movie, music faded in from out of nowhere: *Ground control to Major Tom / Ground control to Major Tom / Take your protein pills and / Put your helmet on.*

The next day, Monday, Wendy wore a tutu to work. She accessorized it with her sharkskin sport jacket slathered with slogan buttons including THERE'S THAT SMELL AGAIN, with three ties, fishnet stockings, and her red hightop Chuck Taylors.

Mr. Boldt was on travel that day.

On Tuesday, Wendy wore a Girl Scout uniform to work, complete with sash and twenty-two badges: sewing, camping, cooking, gardening, animal husbandry. . . . and the THERE'S THAT SMELL AGAIN button.

LBM was still on travel.

On Wednesday—Wendy's last day as a word processor—Little Big Man was back from travel, and Wendy wore the rabbit costume to work. She accessorized the rabbit suit with a wide red cinch belt and a constellation of rhinestone pins, the nucleus of which was the THERE'S THAT SMELL AGAIN button.

Little Big Man didn't come in until noon, and Wendy was on her half-hour lunch break. BG&D had a cafeteria that sold sandwiches and a hot meal, but most of the support staff brought their own lunches. Wendy ate the same thing every day: an iceberg lettuce and American cheese sandwich on white bread, with Miracle Whip and lots of salt and pepper. In the cafeteria, there was an unspoken seating arrangement. The Department of Energy employees — the managers (chiefs they were called) and engineers — sat at the tables in front of the windows, watching the bucolic scene of whitetail deer grazing around the slurry-containment pond. The drones — word processing operators, secretaries, custodians, and maintenance employees — sat in the back.

That day, in her rabbit suit, Wendy took her lettuce and cheese sandwich and sat right down at one of the tables in front of the windows. Roger trailed behind her, wiggling his butt, and sat down across from her. A few of the young male engineers were already seated there.

"So, what's the occasion?" one of them snickered.

"I'm ovulating," Wendy answered, dabbing the corner of her mouth with a paper napkin.

The cafeteria was unusually quiet.

Wendy finished her sandwich, blew up her paper bag, and smacked it against her palm. It made a loud bang, and Roger screamed just as a hand grabbed the back of Wendy's chair.

Behind her stood Little Big Man and a security guard with his hand poised in ready position near his holster, as if the BG&D lunchroom were the O.K. Corral.

"Don't shoot! Don't shoot!" Roger screamed, his hands in the air, his eyes big as pool balls, doing his Buckwheat impersonation.

"You!" Little Big Man shouted at Wendy. "Get up!"

The security officer was another guy named Roger, a white guy with whom Wendy'd had a brief fling years earlier, when she was in college.

Ex-fling Roger took Wendy by the arm, and they walked down the corridor to the exit.

"You don't belong here," he said under his breath as they stepped through the steel door. "They're all assholes," he said. "Uncle Sam is a big asshole."

"Yeah, thanks. I know." Wendy said. "It's just a movie. A 'B' movie."

"More like a 'C' movie."

"An 'F' movie," Wendy said. She was crying. "Like that Gil Scott-Heron song. *Ain't really your life, Ain't really ain't nothing but a movie.*"

"Yeah," White Roger said, as he dutifully scraped the BG&D parking permit off Wendy's windshield. "Happy trails. You can do better than this shit."

"You, too," Wendy said. "Hop in."

Security Roger laughed and shrugged. "I wish . . ." he said wistfully. He was married now with two kids.

Wendy drove along Collins Ferry Road. At the stoplight, a Volvo pulled up beside her, and a toddler who looked like W.C. Fields smiled at her from his car seat and waved his puppet wave. Wendy waved back with her big pink velveteen paw. She looked at herself in the rearview mirror. Her ears were drooping, and she resembled the French lop-eared rabbit, Uncle Wiggily, that her sister and she had when they were kids. As she drove down her narrow alley, a pickup truck parked near the end came into view, and as she got closer, she saw her landlord, Jasper Quince, by her garage apartment, raking leaves.

The curtains on the garage door windows fluttered, and there was William Butler Yeats looking out. Bill's head was so big it was like part of a Chagall painting, one of the ones with a giant chicken, a goat, or a jackass in a suit, interacting with humans.

Wendy would have kept going, but the alley was a cul-de-sac, and Jasper Quince's pickup was blocking the *sac*. Turning around would have required making a K-turn, which Wendy had never mastered. She stopped and turned off the ignition. William Butler Yeats was so happy to see Wendy's car, he started barking for joy. Inside the tiny garage apartment with its aluminum walls, his big bass bark was amplified, like tooting your car horn inside a tunnel. Jasper Quince leaned his rake against the garage, spit a long stream of tobacco juice into the pile of leaves, and walked toward Wendy's car, scowling and adjusting his suspenders.

A rabbit will respond to fear in one of three ways. Usually, when a rabbit is afraid, it remains very still, often holding its breath for an incredibly long time, frozen with fear, catatonic, playing dead. Some rabbits, though, will bolt. The third reaction is attack. Uncle Wiggily, Wendy recalled, was a biter.

✦ Friends Seen and Unseen ✦

Even though she had a handsome, successful husband; a lovely home; and two beautiful children, Marcie often fancied herself living alone. Secretly, she spent a lot of time searching on the Internet for Airstream trailers. Her favorite was the modest yet luxurious Flying Cloud model in the praline color scheme, but even the compact little Bambi would do: something that would fit in the backyard.

A silver bullet.

Marcie lived in Audubon Acres, a gated McMansion community where every street was named after a bird: Goldfinch Circle, Meadowlark Drive, Blackbird Way, Hummingbird Hill. Song birds, pretty birds, pretty names; no Vulture Alley, no Buzzard Circle. Identical brass eagles perched on the stone gateposts leading into Audubon Acres, which those of lesser means referred to as Birdland.

Is it necessary to point out that in Birdland there were no Winnebagos or Airstream campers wintering in backyards or driveways? Why, such plebeian eyesores were against the Birdland property-owners' covenant, just as above-ground pools, outbuildings of any sort, and anything but a certain high-grade of roof shingles within a certain range of subtle earth tones were strictly taboo. Everything uncomely was banished or concealed.

Tyler, Marcie's husband, was a successful businessman who had taken the advice given to Ben Braddock—the Dustin Hoffman character in *The Graduate*. Tyler was in plastics, a high-level sales rep for a plastics extrusion manufacturer with operations in India, China, and Taiwan. He spent a good deal of time in the air. When he was home, he wore a Bluetooth cell phone device curled around his ear, which made his head blink like it was signaling a Kmart special.

Late one night, a month or so after the birth of her eldest son, Finn, Marcie had taken the colicky baby to the rec room so as not to wake Tyler, who had just returned from an extended business trip to Beijing, and it was that night when she came across a made-for-television movie about a Mennonite woman who had been shunned. The punishment for this woman's alleged crime—which was adultery but was never really proven because the woman would neither admit to nor deny the accusation—was that she (her name was Imelda) could never speak to or interact with her family or the Mennonite community again.

But because Mennonites believe in the sanctity of covenants, Imelda remained married to her husband and continued to live as part of the family. So to speak. Her husband, with the help of a few Mennonite friends, converted the one-car garage, which was constructed of concrete block, into an abode for Imelda, installing a small bathroom, an electrical system, and a woodstove. The garage sat behind the house, in the far corner of the backyard, with access from the alley, and from the day of her shunning, that's where Imelda lived.

Imelda's oldest daughter, who was a teenager at the time, took over Imelda's role as mother and assumed the cooking and cleaning and mothering of the three younger children. Every morning and evening, this daughter walked out to Imelda's house with a tray of food and left it atop an upturned milk crate by the door. Imelda ate her meals, washed her dishes, and returned the clean china and silverware to the tray on the stool by the door.

A routine was established. Mother and daughter never spoke.

At night, after the sun set, Imelda could look out her window and, across the expanse of the yard, see the yellow light above the sink in her old kitchen, her daughter preparing dinner, peeling potatoes, snapping beans, setting the table, or doing the dishes, going back and forth behind the window in the soft yellow light, glimpses of her husband from the waist up and the heads of the younger children moving behind her.

Likewise, the daughter could look out and see the yellow light in her mother's tiny house and sometimes her mother herself or her mother's silhouette framed in the window like a *scherenschnitte* paper cutting when the shade was drawn. Sometimes Imelda would wave, and sometimes her daughter would wave back when she was alone in the kitchen, before she turned out the light.

Imelda's house was very small. A hobbit-like dwelling furnished with an old folding metal table and one ladder-back chair; a cot with a deteriorating log-cabin quilt, which Imelda's mother had made; some plastic milk crates in which she stored her belongings; a wicker floor lamp.

In the daytime, Imelda walked to the local library a few blocks away and checked out books: novels, mysteries, romances. She never spoke, and the librarian—another Mennonite—never spoke or made eye contact with Imelda. All day and night, Imelda lay on her cot and read her books, often returning two or three the next day.

Sometimes, very late at night, after all the lights were out in the main house, Imelda went out in the yard and weeded the flower beds and the vegetable garden, plucking a few zinnias to place in a Mason jar, maybe picking an heirloom tomato still warm from the day's heat, and eating it right there in the moonlight, salting it with a shaker she pulled from her cardigan's pocket. Very quietly, she'd straighten up the children's toys, arranging them neatly by the back porch, and usually she unchained the dog, a large mutt with a woolly coat, and brought him into her little house, where he slept on a rag rug by the woodstove until just before dawn.

Sometimes, during the late afternoon when school was over and their father was not yet home, the two youngest children would bravely creep up to Imelda's house and peep in the window, and Imelda would smile and wave and blow them kisses and make the Junior Birdman face for them before pulling down the shade.

The movie ended with a night scene in winter. It was someplace in the Northeast or Midwest maybe—Maine or Wisconsin, perhaps.

Someplace where there's a great deal of snowfall and the drone of snowmobiles can be heard, constantly, in the distance. Big, lazy snowflakes drifted down like flaked coconut, and one by one the lights went out in the neighborhood until all was darkness except for the mullioned rectangle of yellow light that was Imelda's window and a few strands of colored Christmas lights strung tightly around the windows of the two-story frame house.

Slowly, the camera zoomed out, the Christmas lights blinked off, and everything was black except for the little pinprick of Imelda's light as if seen from a satellite in space, the falling snow, and the night, decorated with constellations like a black bandana.

The movie made a strong impression on Marcie as she sat in the rec room late that night nursing and rocking her new baby, trying to quiet him. It was as if Imelda had become an observer rather than a participant in her own life. Almost as if she were a guardian angel, one whose presence was always near and felt and seen even, manifested in the glow of light in the far corner of the backyard. Marcie imagined being one of Imelda's children and what comfort it must have been to know that wherever you were, your mother would always be there in the little house in the backyard, like a shrine with the Blessed Virgin inside. To look out your window at night when you couldn't sleep and see a little glimmer, a little nightlight like one of those canisters with an eternal flame placed on a grave.

Marcie wished that her own mother could have lived in their backyard like Imelda. Instead, Marcie's mother had had eight children and had become a sullen, silent—some even said "crazy"—woman who spent her evenings sitting alone in an overstuffed chair in the cellar, behind the furnace. One Saturday when Marcie was six, after hanging up three loads of laundry, her mother dragged the wing chair out of the living room, kicked it down the basement stairs, and then closed the cellar door.

During the day, Marcie's mother cleaned and cooked. She was a fussy housekeeper—"obsessive compulsive" some would say—and she had taught her children to be mindful of dirt and dust and noise. They were all quiet, well-mannered, neat, reserved, withdrawn children. Likewise, Marcie's father was silent and reserved. He never questioned his wife's retreat to the basement and told the children not to bother her, to just leave their mother alone.

By the time the children came home from school, Marcie's mother had already made her descent, and they knew not to bother her. The beds were made, the laundry was done, the clothes neatly folded and stacked on each family member's bed, the house spotless and orderly. Dinner was prepared, with instructions for cooking printed on a 3 x 5-inch notecard, and the oldest girls served it and tidied up.

They were Catholic.

When Marcie was thirteen, her mother left. Marcie's two older siblings had already gone off, leaving Marcie; her sister Marie, who was one-and-a-half years younger; and three boys, ages ten, seven, and six. The eighth child—the youngest—a girl named Danielle, had died a crib death that same year. She was only eighteen days old.

It was the crib death, people said years later, that had put Marcie's mother "over the edge."

"Your mother's nerves are bad," is all Marcie's father told them when they came home from school one day and their mother was not there, but strangely enough, he was. "She's gone away for a rest," he said.

Later that year, Marcie learned from a classmate that her mother had been committed to a mental hospital. She remained there for two years, receiving electroshock treatments, and when she was released, she went to live with a cousin in another state. These facts Marcie learned years later, after her father had died.

Like the Mennonite couple, Marcie's parents never divorced. Years after her mother's departure, a few months after her father died, Marcie thought she saw her mother downtown. She caught a glimpse of a woman outside Family Dollar as she was driving down High Street. Twenty-one years had passed since she'd seen her mother, and although the woman in front of Family Dollar was bundled in lumpy clothing like Marcie had never seen her mother wear, and although her hair was covered with a scarf and her face averted, and although Marcie observed her from a distance, something about the woman's presence—her carriage—reminded Marcie immediately of her mother. She was certain it was her.

Marcie drove around the block to get a better look, but by then, the woman had disappeared. Marcie parked her car and went in Family Dollar, walking up and down the glaring aisles, trembling, but the woman was not there. Still, the figure of the woman haunted her. She saw her in dreams and more than once, while in the basement doing laundry, Marcie saw her mother peep out from behind the furnace. On several occasions her mother spoke, offering matter-of-fact advice on stain removal and child rearing.

"Use the Tide stick first," her mother would instruct, and when discussing Marcie's son Finn, her mother's advice was, "Don't let him get the best of you."

Family Dollar had been the old F.W. Woolworth store, with its long lunch counter in the front; a big, red, boisterous peanut roaster dead center; and screaming birds and frantic hamsters caged in the stinky pet department in the back. Although the store was greatly changed—rather pitifully so—the façade remained basically the same, and Family Dollar still had the old tattered striped awning from its Woolworth's days. Even back then, the front of the store attracted local characters who took shelter from the elements in the umbra of the Woolworth's awning.

Back when Marcie was little—back in the '70s—her mother always gave her and her siblings each a quarter to buy a pencil from Sombrero Man, who was stationed outside Woolworth's rain or shine, hot or cold. As the sobriquet implied, Sombrero Man wore an enormous Mexican sombrero. His was black and adorned with gold braid and the remains of glittery stars and green felt saguaro cacti, the brim dangling a row of dirty, unevenly spaced, moth-eaten pinkish-red globs like half-sucked Atomic Fireballs. In the winter, Sombrero Man was wrapped in army blankets and wore fingerless rag gloves. Sombrero Man had no legs and navigated via a wooden cart like Porgy in *Porgy & Bess*. Marcie was afraid of him because of his deformity, but her mother made each of them approach him, drop their coin in his hand, and say thank you for the No. 2 yellow pencil he handed them.

TICONDEROGA, the pencils said.

Like its predecessor, Family Dollar still attracted weirdoes and street people. It was a good location, right on a busy corner with a lengthy traffic light, a crosswalk, and a bus stop. Sombrero Man was long dead, and Small Appliance had taken over his spot. Small Appliance was a tubby, mentally challenged, middle-aged man who always held a toaster, a blender, an electric beater, a Dustbuster, a Mr. Coffee, a crockpot, a fondue pot, an incomplete set of electric rollers, or some other small appliance clutched to his chest like a teddy bear. Small Appliance never spoke. He got off the southside bus every morning and stood in front of Family Dollar all day, hugging his small appliance, just staring blankly into space and humming the theme song from *Bonanza*.

The corner of High and Walnut—in front of Family Dollar—was a good place to run up to cars, too, and wipe their windshields with a rag, smiling, wild-eyed, right in the drivers' faces, while they sat in traffic. Swiping and wiping and smiling, even after the light had changed, swiping and wiping and smiling . . . until you got a quarter. That was what Car Wash did.

And then there was Q-Tip, the tall, chopstick-thin black man with the enormous white Afro.

And then there was Zero and his little dog, Lucky. Zero was a prophet.

"Friends seen and unseen . . ." all of Prophet Zero's "transmissions" began . . .

> You who are toolin' along in your SUV automobiles . . .
>
> You who are a-talkin' and a-textin' on your Blackberries . . .
>
> You who are groovin' to your iTunes and your "Car Talk" and your "Prairie Home Companion," and your "All Things Considered" . . .
>
> You who are boarding your omnibuses with your push-button, collapsible umbrellas and your genuine cowhide water-repellant briefcases . . .
>
> You with your grandé mocha caramel cinnamon soy skinny lattés with whipped cream on top, looking down on us

from the great heights of buildings and airplanes and beyond;

You who are lying in your gutters with your cardboard and your angels and your demons huddled there beside you . . .

You with your pretty pink go-go boots and your big Jackie O shades—you lookin' soooooo good . . .

You with your pinstriped silk Armani tie looped around your neck like a noose . . .

You with that death grip on your shiny black pocketbook clutched against your bosom like it might snap open its big maw and SCREEEEEEAM if you let go . . .

Listen up, you childs of the universe, you childs of light and dung and unknown particles . . . you with your alcohol and your mercury and your nicotine and your antidepressants and your Xanax and your cocaine and your maryjane and your oxycontin and your dioxin and your crystal meth and your ginkgo biloba coursin' through your veins:

Prophet Zero and the Family of Light loves you all! And we greets you with the holy word, "Yo!"

Yo!

Prophet Zero was a rubbery-limbed guy with wild grizzled hair breaking out from a mangy buffalo-plaid fur-lined cap with earflaps. He had a bushy beard that matched his hair and gave the impression that he was really just a big hairball with a circle buzzed away to expose a face. Prophet Zero wore raggedy clothes, puffs of stuffing poking out of big rips in his quilted nylon ski jacket. His clothes were so torn and tattered, Prophet Zero looked like a big, grungy dog toy that a Jack Russell had tried to rip the squeaker out of. And succeeded.

But despite his ragtag appearance, Prophet Zero was a magnificent homespun orator. A natural. The timbre of his voice was gentle, yet it carried far, like ragweed pollen: a rich, melodious Barry White baritone that penetrated—without shouting—the cacophony of traffic and horns, air compressors and jackhammers, and his sermons displayed an extemporaneous eloquence as he reached into the urban seamonster and plucked out details that shimmered like pearls, his voice full of fervor and mirth, never rage.

Rage: it was the Achilles' heel of other street prophets, who alienated commuters with their raves and condemnations. But Zero's message was joyous, and it was fun to be singled out of the masses by Prophet Zero—to be chosen—as he picked out your Hermes scarf or your Carhartt jacket, spreading goodwill like mayonnaise. Instead of fire and brimstone, Prophet Zero's transmissions were more like a combination of pot and Red Bull. Cotton Mather on Quaaludes. Ardent beneficence.

And Zero could play the harmonica, too, play it like Sonny Boy Williamson, John Mayall, James Cotton, Bob Dylan, sometimes sticking half the harp in his mouth and playing it without his hands, playing a medley that wove strands of the doxology with "Two Trains Runnin'," "Room to Move," and "All Along the Watch Tower."

Together, Prophet Zero and Lucky, Car Wash, Q-Tip, and Small Appliance were known as "the Family." They were a harmless bunch, and Dennis W., the Family Dollar manager, treated them well, never shooing them away or calling the police, and often giving them things: a yellow Family Dollar plastic bag with damaged canned goods like tuna and Spam, Ritz Crackers and Fruit Loops with expired sell-by dates, mutilated Chunkies and Squirrel Nut Caramels, shelf-worn toiletries and clothing and always, a box of puppy-size Milk Bone dog biscuits for Lucky, and maybe a bottle of Windex thrown in for Car Wash and a chintzy electric can opener for Small Appliance.

The Family was sometimes joined by a woman who stood by the Family Dollar entrance and held out a chipped earthenware dog bowl as a collection plate for Zero. Having designated herself the official Family Dollar greeter, she held the door for customers and chimed, "Thank you for shopping Family Dollar. Have a beautiful, beautiful day," as she held out the dog bowl with the name LATKE stenciled on it. The greeter was known as Angel.

"Yo!" Zero would call out, greeting cars and pedestrians.

"Yo!" strangers would call back, tip their hats, wave.

In imitation of Zero, "Yo!" had become a standard form of greeting in the law office where Marcie worked, one block up High and two blocks west on Walnut, toward the river.

"Yo!" the young student intern would greet Marcie every morning when he burst in, hung up his pea coat, and stuck his head in her cubicle, "you in your beautiful blue cashmere sweater, you with your beautiful blue eyes, you who are typing that crummy brief. Nate greets you with the holy word, Yo!"

And if the coast was clear, he'd steal a kiss.

Nate's impersonation of Zero was right-on: fluent and charming. Nate was a third-year law student, interning with Bowles Rice & Bean, where Marcie was a paralegal, and although he was ten years Marcie's junior, there was an immediate attraction between them from the first day of his internship—a sexual attraction—and from the moment of that first introduction, Marcie found herself taking special care with her clothes and her hair, in anticipation of seeing Nate; daydreaming of him during the day, and imagining him next to her at night instead of Tyler.

She began to wear perfume.

A harmless flirtation, she told herself.

Marcie was married. With children. Nate was "involved," as he put it.

But because, possibly, there is no such thing as a harmless flirtation, said harmless flirtation escalated into an affair, complete with the requisite deception and furtive sex. And because of the frequency and duration of Tyler's travels, trysting opportunities abounded, and the affair flourished. For three months, that is, until the day Nate announced casually to the entire Bowles Rice & Bean staff (including Marcie, of course) during their Thanksgiving luncheon, that he'd just gotten engaged.

Nate's fiancé, Giselle—Gizzy, for short—was a dancer. One of those grown women with a woman's face and the peculiar tiny, flat-chested body of a ten-year-old, the ram-rod posture of a molded plastic doll. Something about her appearance was unnerving—like a little girl in lipstick and mascara, like JonBenét Ramsey. Gizzy had a sharp, prominent nose and close-set eyes and wore her thick hair pulled back tightly in a severe bun, which she had a habit of undoing and redoing and undoing again, twisting and wrapping and tucking the cloth band around and around her auburn tresses as she talked, always with perfect posture, always pointing her toes or moving her slippered feet between first, second, and third position. And in spite of the fact that Gizzy was unequivocally beautiful, Marcie (who was full figured) was able to convince herself that Gizzy looked like a sparrow hawk or some exotic rodent. Such is the power of delusion, the power of self-deception, the power of love.

Nate's casual announcement at the catered lunch, after his having spent most of the previous night with Marcie, was nothing short of devastating.

Finn, Marcie's oldest boy, was six, and he called Prophet Zero the Yo-Man. "Yo!" Finn would holler when they walked by Prophet Zero downtown. He'd pet Zero's little dog, Lucky, who'd jump in the air and spin.

"Yo, little man!" Zero would call back, "you with your supercool Spider Man backpack."

Finn was a precocious child. *Too smart for his own good,* Marcie thought. *Too big for his breeches.* He was demanding and, even at age six, arrogant. "Yo! Mommy, get me a juice box," or "Yo! Mommy . . ." followed by buy me this or buy me that.

"Don't talk to me like that," Marcie would scold him. "Say, 'Mommy, please, may I . . .'"

And Finn would ignore her or stick out his tongue.

He was often destructive and exhibited neither signs of remorse for the toys he destroyed nor any change of behavior after the mild punishment he received: time-out in his room, no television.

Marcie tried to talk to Tyler about him.

"The kid's got spunk!" Tyler said proudly. "Leave him alone, Marcie. You're going to turn him into some pussy-whipped mama's boy." Or, "Leave him alone, Marcie. He'll outgrow this. It's just a phase. Dwelling on it is just reinforcing the undesirable behavior."

But, of course, Tyler was hardly ever home. And when he was, he pampered the boy, lavishing him with gifts—Matchbox cars, remote control airplanes, GameBoys or some other electronic toy knockoff purchased cheaply in China or Taiwan. His briefcase always held a box of

Good & Plenty or Tootsie Roll Pops. And they were always going off together—just the two of them—while Marcie stayed home with the baby.

The baby—Davitt—though, was sweet, affectionate, and cheerful, with a soft yellow tuft of hair on his head like a chick. He had not yet acquired language, which was a good thing, Marcie thought, because who knew what he'd grow up to say, and at thirteen months, he was still a babbler and a drooler. And he was anything but demanding. He was content to amuse himself in the playpen, swing, or walker. Marcie rarely spoke to him, yet he babbled to himself and sometimes squealed with pure delight. He was more like having a dear pet around. Except for the diapers and feedings. A dear sick pet, perhaps.

After Finn's birth, Marcie had fallen into a deep depression. Dark, inky shadows stained the papery skin around her eyes. She couldn't concentrate, couldn't sleep, and she felt anxious and exhausted all the time. She had nightmares and dreadful thoughts. She was deeply embarrassed about feeling despondent at a time when everyone expected her to be blissful and elated. Observing the bruise-like shadows under her eyes, a co-worker even went so far as to take her aside and ask her if someone had hit her, insinuating domestic violence.

"The Baby Blues," her OB-GYN explained casually, writing her a prescription for an antidepressant and another for an anti-anxiety drug. "Nothing to fret about.

"It's not uncommon," he continued reassuringly. "It's perfectly normal to feel blue after giving birth. It's hormonal. After childbirth, a woman's hormones are raging, but like a hurricane, this too shall pass. For some women, it's worse than for others. Don't despair," he said, patting Marcie's knee. "Come back and see me in eight weeks."

And he was right. The drugs helped, and in a few months Marcie was feeling better.

But after Davitt's birth, the depression returned, this time deeper, and the prescriptions didn't help, although Marcie kept taking them, and out of weariness and embarrassment, she lied to the doctor about their effectiveness. It was during this time that Marcie began to fantasize about the Airstream trailer and to think about her mother and Imelda. Sometimes Marcie's mother came and stood behind her in Tyler's study as

Marcie surfed the Internet late at night when she couldn't sleep. Together, Marcie and her mother weighed the pros and cons of one particular Airstream model over another. Like Marcie, her mother preferred the streamlined Flying Cloud, and together they discussed its specifications and options. Perhaps they would go off together some day, visiting state parks and the ocean.

With every passing day, Marcie saw more of his father in Finn. Arrogance. Pride. These two qualities seemed to inflate in Tyler with every accomplishment, every promotion. Finn was just like his father. He was a little know-it-all. His father was a big know-it-all.

Finn had an imaginary friend he called Tripkin. Marcie hated Tripkin. When Tripkin first entered the picture—right before Davitt was born—everyone—including Marcie—thought that Finn was so cute and imaginative, but Tripkin turned out to be a little monster, assuming all of Finn's undesirable traits and manifesting them all the time.

"Mommy," Finn might say, "Tripkin says there's no reason for me to go to bed so early. Tripkin says you're manipulating me." Or, "Mommy, Tripkin says you're fat. Tripkin says you're mean. Tripkin says you're ugly."

"Tripkin needs his mouth washed out with soap," Marcie said.

"Tripkin likes soap in his mouth," Finn replied.

And then it would begin: the battle of wills. With Finn usually winning, Marcie too exhausted to carry on.

When he was frustrated and intentionally broke something—usually something of Marcie's—Finn claimed that Tripkin did it. When at school he'd pushed a little girl off of a swing, causing her to break her wrist, he said it wasn't him; it was Tripkin did the pushing.

A parent-teacher conference was scheduled. The conference was the same afternoon as the luncheon when Nate announced his engagement to Gizzy. During the luncheon, someone ran to the wine shop across the street and bought two bottles of champagne, and everyone raised a glass and toasted Nate and his fiancée. "Yo," someone said, "Yo, to you, with your beautiful new bride-to-be."

Marcie tried to still her nerves and slipped off to the bathroom, where she took two Xanax, washing them down with her glass of champagne. At 3:30, she excused herself, leaving work early for the parent-teacher conference.

"You know about this Tripkin, this imaginary friend of Finn's, Mrs. Hobarth?" the teacher asked.

"Yes."

"And what do you make of him . . . it . . .?" the teacher asked. Across the desk she handed Marcie a drawing. A child's drawing of some kind of sinister creature with horns, a Lone Ranger mask, a large mouth with bright red lips and too many teeth, a crocodile tail.

"What's this?" Marcie asked, trying to sound incredulous, but she already knew. She'd seen this likeness before. Only something in this particular drawing caught her eye. Tripkin was carrying a brown box that could not be construed as anything but a briefcase.

"Mrs. Hobarth, this is Finn's drawing of Tripkin. Our school counselor, Mr. Wyslowski, who is trained as an art therapist, thinks Finn is troubled. Is there something wrong at home? Has he exhibited any unusual behavior, any acting out? We would like him to be evaluated."

Marcie remained silent.

"With your permission, Mrs. Hobarth, we'll begin testing him on Monday, if you'll sign this release form. The results of the tests will, of course, be confidential, and they'll help us identify any—"

"Of course," Marcie said, picking up the pen.

A half-hour later, Marcie pulled up to the curb, joining the long, curved spine of the segmented serpent waiting to swallow the children from the afterschool Boys and Girls Club. Davitt was asleep, buckled and slumped into his car seat after his day at Teddy Bear Cove.

At exactly 4:20 p.m., the double doors opened and the children poured out. There was Finn in his bright blue, puffy jacket, lagging behind alone, shuffling, stooped under his ugly red Spiderman pack that covered his back like a turtle's shell. Only 4:30 p.m., and already it was getting dark, and the solstice still almost a month away. Snow was forecast for the weekend, starting that evening and accumulating up to twelve inches in the higher elevations. The long winter stretched before them. After the solstice, it would start going the other way: a little more light earlier each morning and lingering into the evening. And then the burst of spring: bright shoots of crocuses and daffodils, redbuds, the brave little snowdrops foolishly exposing their tender blossoms along the front walk. Maybe then, Marcie and her mother would hit the road.

Leaving town, heading toward Audubon Acres, the traffic was heavy and backed up, the cars and trucks creeping slowly along the highway, which was slick with freshly fallen snow, the salt trucks not yet out and about. It was Wednesday evening, the day before Thanksgiving. Many people were leaving town, and others—sports fans—were beginning to descend on the city for the university's first basketball game of the season.

There were still some last-minute things to be picked up at Giant Eagle: another bag of cranberries, prepared horseradish, another bottle of prosecco. The stuffing had to be made: all that chopping and mixing. And the pies. Leaves to be put in the table. The turkey to be washed and prepped for roasting, the reaching inside the cavity and pulling out the slippery bag of giblets—the liver, heart, and neck. If she hadn't spent last night with Nate—.

Tyler would be arriving about now at Pittsburgh International Airport from Taipei. Would his flight be delayed? And tomorrow, Marcie's in-laws—Tyler's parents and his brother and family—were coming for dinner.

So much to do.

But with this weather, would anybody make it?

From the backseat, Finn began to pester her. "Tripkin doesn't want to go home," Finn whined, "Tripkin wants pizza."

Marcie stared at the road and tried to concentrate. She didn't answer.

"Tripkin wants pizza," Finn insisted. "Tripkin wants pizza. Tripkin wants pizza. Tripkin wants pizza. Tripkin wants pizza. Tripkin wants pizza," he chanted.

Marcie didn't answer.

"Don't let him get the best of you," her mother reminded her. Marcie's mother sat beside her, dressed in a bulky tweed coat and blue fuzzy hat.

"Turn here," Marcie's mother said a few miles later, pointing to a sign on the interstate one exit before the Audubon Acres one. "Take the back road."

"Good idea," Marcie said. Her mother smiled reassuringly.

The back road was old Route 73, which wound down the mountain and around the lake toward the old iron bridge.

Just before the bridge, a service road leading to the old boat launch veered off, and Marcie turned as her mother instructed. Marcie hadn't been down there in years, not since she was a teenager and had gone there with friends on summer nights to skinny dip, drink beer around a bonfire, and make out. A boy in her graduating class had drowned there, diving from the pinnacle of the bridge.

A warning sign was spray-painted over, tagged with a strange, elaborately knotted glyph. The road was rutted and bumpy, washed out in places, steep and slick. Spears of sumac jabbed and scraped the car.

Marcie kept driving, right down to the end of the road, to the boat launch, and parked.

The sun was setting, and the cold gray lake flashed like a cookie sheet in the last blaze of sunset.

Marcie turned off the car, and she and her mother got out. As Marcie locked the doors with her clicker, a rowdy flock of migrating Canadian geese milled around the edge of the lake, squawking, protesting the invasion of Marcie's Explorer. One of the ganders waddled toward her, screaming and flapping his wings belligerently. "Go back! Get outta here!" he was saying. Another day, another life, Marcie might have laughed at his pathetic tough-guy display. He walked like a toddler with a load in his pants.

"Mommy!" Finn hollered from inside the car, banging on the window, "Tripkin says we should go home now. Mommy! Tripkin says —"

Marcie looked back. The dome light was still on, and she could see Finn's angry little face, his small fist like a rubber mallet banging on the window, his red mouth moving behind the glass, which was rapidly steaming up. The snow was coming down steadily, the temperature falling.

"Yo, Mommy!" Finn hollered again, banging harder on the window this time.

"Yo," Baby Davitt chimed in, gaily slapping the plastic steering wheel attached to his car seat. "Yo-yo-yo-yo-yo-yo. . . ." he smiled and babbled as Marcie waved to him one last time. The ground was slippery, a stiff glaze of snow like boiled icing poured over a mush of rotting sycamore leaves. Marcie kept walking, wobbling and slipping in her high-heeled boots, following her mother to the bridge.

✦ The Old Laughing Lady ✦

Very slowly, Bunny had been working through the stages of grief like Elisabeth Kübler-Ross's book instructed, but she seemed to have been stuck in the anger phase for an inordinately long time: twelve years. And anger was only the second phase of the grief-recovery process.

The first phase of grief—disbelief—she shot right through like Secretariat. In fact, that phase had only lasted a minute or so, if that. As soon as Gerald told Bunny that he was leaving her for his surgical nurse, Connie Simmons, Bunny believed it. Oh, she believed it, all right. She didn't *disbelieve* it for one minute. She'd always suspected that there was some hanky-panky going on between the two of them. What she hadn't suspected was that that something between them included two children.

And so the news came as a deadly two-stroke blow to Bunny, who was left grieving not just for the death of her long marriage but for the children she never had, the children who Gerald had led her to believe he was *incapable* of fathering.

What a prick! There she was, suddenly divorced at age forty-five. And childless. And where was Gerald? Relocated to Florida with his new bride and two adolescent children.

Bunny and Gerald had been married nearly fifteen years when Gerald made his little announcement, shortly after Connie's husband—Gerald's colleague, Rory Simmons—died. Of course, there was no way Gerald was going to make that move while Rory was still alive. Rory Simmons was the head of Cardiology, and Gerald's ass would have been grass, so to speak, if Connie had left Rory for Gerald when Rory was still alive. And so Gerald and Connie had carried on a twelve-year affair—through four-fifths of Bunny's marriage.

What a damn piece of genetic good luck for Connie and Gerald that Rory—like Gerald—was a redhead. Otherwise, how could Connie have explained those redheaded children? Connie was olive skinned and dark complected and had a nose like a plantain. Ansel and Agnes—names that sounded to Bunny like cattle raised by 4-H Club adolescents—were Connie and Gerald's spawn. They both had inherited their mother's proboscis, and their hair was their next most prominent feature, so they looked a perfect Simmons family fit: big nose, red hair. That Connie, she had all the bases covered.

So now Connie and Gerald were together, living the good life, Bunny supposed, in the Sunshine State, and Bunny was still stuck in West Virginia in the damn geodesic dome she and Gerald had built.

Bunny never wanted the dome, but Gerald was a big Buckminster Fuller fan back then, and he was the breadwinner, and back in those early days of their marriage, Bunny wasn't very assertive. She was docile and impressionable, and she went along with everything, always deferring to Gerald. She was a people pleaser. It was her nature.

That was the old days.

The dome looked like a giant, half-buried golf ball. It was built from a kit, constructed with a metal frame and fitted with prefabricated, triangular steel-reinforced building blocks, and then stuccoed. In their established neighborhood, amidst the Victorian Painted Ladies and the early twentieth-century bungalows and four-squares, the dome was as out-of-place as a disco ball in a Friends meeting house. Neighbors were at first just inquisitive, then appalled, as they watched the new construction take shape.

Even before its completion, the dome was a joke. It was a local landmark. "Go to the golf ball, and turn right on Grant Avenue." Standard directions for navigating through Sunnyside. Or people chanted, "In Sunnyside did Dr. Wells a geodesic dome decree."

And no amount of landscaping could obscure it.

Kudzu was the only answer.

And although Gerald always lauded Buckminster Fuller's design, as a house the dome was a fiasco. The dome was drafty, dark, and damp; hard to heat, hard to illuminate. Impossible to decorate. And it leaked like a lace umbrella. It had too few windows, too little headroom in most places, too much in the middle, and since the day she moved in, Bunny had always felt like she was walking around in circles. And she was.

But Gerald stuck to his guns and would not abandon it.

So, of course, in the divorce settlement, Bunny got Goliath's golf ball. She tried to sell it. Nobody wanted it. After a few years on the market, she gave up and planted kudzu. How many people have actually *planted* kudzu? Bunny wondered. But it worked. After a few years, swaddled in kudzu, the geodesic dome no longer looked like an enormous golf ball but more like a curious landform. A terrestrial goiter.

The only problem with the kudzu, aside from the fact that she had to constantly hack it away from the entryways and windows, like a character out of *One Hundred Years of Solitude* fighting back the Colombian jungle, was that it was taking over the neighborhood. The kudzu was so invasive that after a few years, the neighborhood looked like a set for *Sleeping Beauty*. The kudzu crept for blocks and blocks up and down Bunny's side of the street—scampering across lawns and up trees, throwing itself like an afghan over fences, girding buildings, fringing utility lines, all with the stealth and speed of a virus. Based on Bunny's landscaping, a city ordinance against introducing kudzu had been passed, and it was illegal now to plant or propagate it. Everybody in the neighborhood hated Bunny and called her Kudzulla.

Except Edna. Edna was ninety-two years old and lived next door and just didn't give a shit about the kudzu. In fact, Edna thought the kudzu rather nice. "Enchanting," she said. Edna's Victorian brick house, like Bunny's geodesic dome, was covered with kudzu, but she was the only person in the neighborhood who supported Bunny's landscaping.

Every day, after lopping away the kudzu that grew during the night around her own front door, Bunny went next door to Edna's house with her loppers and did the same. And then, over a cup of decaffeinated organic oolong tea, she read aloud the obituaries and the front page of the local paper. The obituaries always came first because both women awoke with a curiosity as to who was still on earth and who had crossed over. That web of human things.

And so it was at Edna's house that Bunny learned of Connie's death. "After a lengthy illness," the obituary said, "Mrs. Connie Wells of Palm Beach, Florida, formerly of Morgantown—"

"That means cancer," Edna interrupted, sipping her tea. "She should have taken the vinegar cure."

The obituary included a photograph of Connie taken probably thirty years earlier, with her dark hair in an exaggerated flip like Mary Tyler Moore on *The Dick Van Dyke Show*, and sporting cat-eye glasses, which appeared to shorten her nose, drawing attention away from her schnozzola to her Neanderthalish forehead. It was a flattering photo, Bunny had to admit. The photographer had probably positioned the glasses halfway down the bridge of Connie's nose to achieve the desired effect.

Connie, the obituary stated, was fifty, seven years younger than Bunny. She was preceded in death by her first husband, Dr. Rory Simmons, and survived by her second husband, Dr. Gerald Wells, and their children, Ansel and Agnes, their spouses and three grandchildren. There was a website address to send condolences.

Bunny's anger could erupt at any time, in any place, as unpredictably as a volcano in a Mexican cornfield. Kübler-Ross said that you had to let go of the anger, move past it, but Bunny couldn't. It lay buried deep inside her like a hairball she could never fully regurgitate. Her anger about Gerald's betrayal and the resentment she harbored toward Connie could manifest over the slightest annoyance. She lashed out at people over trivial things—in the faculty lounge, in the grocery store check-out line, in traffic, in class. The slightest annoyance exploded into a confrontation. All of her outbursts were inappropriate expressions of the coagulated glob of anger she couldn't expel. She was frustrated and bitter, and this negativity had cost her innumerable friendships.

People—people who used to like her—couldn't stand to be around her anymore. Once a popular teacher, enrollment in the one graduate-level English course she now taught—"Survey of Medieval, Renaissance, Seventeenth Century, Eighteenth Century, Nineteenth Century, and Twentieth Century British Literature"—had dwindled.

Yes, it was one of only two literature offerings in the graduate program. (The other was its American counterpart.) Yes, Donne, Bacon, Tennyson, Lawrence, Chaucer, Austen, the Eliots, Shakespeare, Milton, Marvell, the Herberts, Herrick, Lovelace, Suckling, Wordsworth, Blake, Yeats, Woolf, Jonson, Trollope, Fielding, Waugh, Thackeray, Swift, Dickens, Forster, Gissing, Shelley, Keats, Byron, the Venerable Bede, and all the rest had all been tossed and squashed and rolled into one three-credit crash course. And, yes, English PhD candidates were more familiar with Harry Potter than Hamlet and could quote Homer Simpson but not the Holy Sonnets.

One by one, the Old Guard—the critical mass of true scholars of literature in the English Department—was retiring, and the canon had been usurped by the Red Pens, the postmodernists, deconstructionists, and diversitists, the theory dogs, identity politicians and pop culture critics, and, worst of all: the creative writers. Oh, the creative writers in their BE CAREFUL WHAT YOU SAY. YOU MIGHT END UP IN MY NOVEL/MEMOIR/POEM/SHORT STORY t-shirts! The creative writers with their mantras, "Show, Don't Tell!" and "Write What You Know!" The creative writers, always scribbling away in their little Moleskines and running off to their little colonies and giving their precious little readings at Barnes & Noble, introducing each other and calling one another "luminous," "visionary," and "brave" (to their faces). Thank gawd for blenders and cappuccino machines. Bunny always ordered a smoothie *and* a grandé latté whenever she happened into the bookstore during one of their readings.

Twice Bunny had been reprimanded by the department chair. The first incident took place in one of Bunny's classes where every discussion was dominated by an arrogant graduate student who spewed forth convoluted, pseudo-intellectual drivel from the Emperor's Old Deconstructionist, Jacques Derrida. Finally, halfway into the semester, Bunny threw up her arms in the middle of one of this student's monologues and screamed, "But you have nothing to say!" The student ran to the chair, crying, "Rude! Disrespectful! Bully!" The second reprimand came during a curriculum meeting when Bunny proposed that all literature courses be combined into one three-credit pass/fail elective wherein students would study jacket copy. "Great Blurbs," the course would be called.

When a bright yellow flier appeared in her mailbox announcing that the English Department's distinguished lecture series would be kicked off by a talk on "Polyvalence and Factography in Contemporary Anti-Hegemonic and Synecdochic Discourses that Disambiguate Generic and Canonical Forms," Bunny had the flier enlarged to poster size and laminated, and then tacked it on her office door. The following week, one of her students turned in a "critical paper" comparing the hairdos of five authors on the *New York Times* bestseller list.

Bunny tried to let it all wash over her, but she couldn't. She was never promoted to the rank of full professor. She became an isolated and glum, middle-aged, post-menopausal woman who surrounded herself with cats. After every disappointment, Bunny drove to the local animal shelter and brought home a cat on death row. She was up to twelve, all of them named after Shakespearean characters—Peaseblossom, Cobweb, Mote, and Mustardseed; Bottom, Quince, Puck, and Snout; Hippolyta, Oberon, Titania, and Lysander. Another neighborhood concern. And there were rumors of imminent animal-control stings in Sunnyside with regard to the ordinance that limited the number of domestic animals that could be kept at any one residence at one time within the city limits. Quadruple-digit fines per offense, impoundment, incarceration. Publicity. Shame.

And while the city fathers concerned themselves with vines and felines, zoning variances were doled out like Halloween candy, and the neighborhood was going to pot with rampant, unregulated development in the form of massive, ugly, poorly constructed student housing and the continued conversion of single-family dwellings into multifamily student housing units.

Things had been going on in the neighborhood, things Bunny just couldn't tolerate. That hideous and huge student apartment building—the one everyone called "The Kennels"—behind her house—and with a liquor store on the first floor: was that inviting drunkenness and wantonness, or what? Who would want their children to live there, even if it was within easy commuting distance to both campuses? And that dirty bookstore next door to it: the Adult Toy Box. Men furtively coming and going all hours of the day, chins tucked, eyes averted, gaits expedient, black plastic bags tucked under their arms.

And they had no business converting the old A&P into a bar/ nightclub, and now there was trouble with this new place, this Club Z. What did the "Z" stand for anyway? Just yesterday, the front page headline was about another "incident"—a drunken brawl—outside Club Z. One man had been stabbed and was in critical condition in Mon General, and three men had been arrested.

The latest development was the profane transformation of the Cassuccio house across the street into a student rental. Florentino and Antoinetta Cassuccio had come to Morgantown in the late 1940s from Italy, newlyweds. Florentino was a skilled stonemason and had built their home entirely from stones he found in the surrounding area. Every evening he roamed the neighborhood with his wheelbarrow, returning home with it full of rocks. He finished the house in 1950, and while building it, he and Antoinetta lived in the cellar. The house had hardwood floors, chestnut woodwork and plaster walls, three bedrooms, and a tile bathroom, all built and finished inside and out by Florentino himself. But Florentino and Antoinetta never moved upstairs from the basement. For fifty-five years, they continued to live underground, entering and exiting the house by the steel doors that opened like a hatch onto steep cement steps that led into the cellar.

Every day Antoinetta went upstairs, dusted, swept, vacuumed, scrubbed and waxed the floors, and polished the windows with newspaper and vinegar. The 1950s furniture was still covered in the original plastic slipcovers when the house was sold in 2006, after Antoinetta died at age ninety-eight. The kitchen appliances were vintage 1950s, shiny and immaculate; they'd never been used. All year round, every year, every day, until the year before she took ill and died, Antoinetta climbed out of a second-story bedroom window and swept the porch roof. The house was a museum, testimony to their industry and success in the New World, where they both had worked six days a week for over forty years, she in the Bailey Glass factory, he as a bricklayer and stonemason.

But now the Cassuccio's home was owned by an absentee slumlord who rented it to six male university students who hung a Confederate flag in the picture window and drug the pristine 1950s mohair couch out to the front porch, where they tapped a new keg of beer nearly every evening. The disrespect was criminal, and the house overflowed with revelers, people of all ages and descriptions, students and otherwise, coming and going night and day at party central.

And late every night—around 11:00 p.m.—the altercations started, the yelling *Fuck you! Oh yeah? Well, fuck you! Fuck you! Fuck you! Fuck you!* Shattering glass, screeching cars, police sirens, spinning blue lights, angry voices. More *Fuck you! Fuck you! Fuck you!*

"Can't they think of anything more interesting to shout than *Fuck you?*" Edna remarked. "What about Shakespearean insults?"

And Bunny had to laugh. No doubt the most successful, rewarding experience of her long teaching career had been the class where she'd taught twentysome teenage hooligans at a youth detention center how to curse in Elizabethan English. They were a tough bunch, and after three classes of plowing through *Julius Caesar*, Bunny came up with the idea of Elizabethan expletives and slurs. They had a grand old time of it, and Bunny remembered laughing from her belly like she'd never laughed before. She'd made a table with four columns, the first three a list of modifiers, the last column a list of nouns. What you had to do was preface your insult with "Thou" or "A pox on your house, thou . . ." or "Die and be damned, thou . . ." and then pick a word from each column.

She could still see their laughing faces. Sometimes, even recently, she recognized some of their names in the daily report, names she'd never forget: Sympathy Allegra Jakes: forgery and possession of a controlled substance with intent to sell; LaFontaine Rose: breaking and entering; Boze Ramone: assault with a deadly weapon.

But that day, that day they were not just adjudicated youth, many of them more familiar with the beige and institutional green walls and locked windows of the Kennedy Youth Center than with the place they called home. That day, they were just kids, venting their anger in Elizabethan English, having fun.

This was just before "The Blow," and that night in bed Bunny recounted to Gerald the hysterical curses the kids had shouted to each other. The bed shook with Bunny and Gerald's laughter, and at one point, Gerald laughed so hard, he almost choked.

Ah, if only he had, Bunny mused.

Edna was the only person who hadn't given Bunny the brush. Partly because Bunny was nearly indispensable to her. Bunny took Edna grocery shopping at Giant Eagle and to her doctor's appointments; she was always doing things for Edna, and in Edna's presence, Bunny was her old self, not the angry, confrontational person she'd become. There was something about being needed, something about living up to another person's expectations that made her step outside herself and, for the moment at least, assume the projected identity.

And really, Edna truly liked Bunny. Bunny was a lot like her, only Edna had somehow succeeded in working through her own anger and living a life of peace. She, too, had lived through a long, unhappy marriage, but at the age of forty-nine, she'd divorced her philandering husband and, with only one suitcase and $200, boarded a train to New York City, setting out for a life of her own—without a job, without even a place to stay.

She ended up at the YWCA, and eventually, as the executive director of the American Association of Professional Women, and from there, the sky was the limit. Edna traveled around the world, and she fell in love with a woman, a female osteopath, fifteen years her senior, and lived with her for eighteen years—until her companion's death—before moving back to Morgantown, to the house she'd grown up in. She told all this openly to Bunny, never denying her sexual orientation or the long, circuitous road to embracing it. To Bunny, Edna was a marvel, and only in Edna's presence did Bunny momentarily let go of her anger. Why? Because Edna didn't want to hear it. When Bunny embarked on one of her tirades or self-pity parties, Edna advised her to "let it go."

"Dear," she'd remind her again and again, "it was for the best. One day you'll jump and shout about it. Believe me. Just give it time. Give it up."

And she never failed to greet Bunny with genuine happiness and kindest regard. Edna's door was always open to Bunny, even late at night. Edna, in fact, was a night owl. Some elderly people, it seemed, slept all the time. But some, like Edna, rarely slept. It was how the body absorbed and used time, Edna said. If you slept a lot, you used time up, and time diminished. If you stayed awake, time expanded. Edna stayed awake most of the day and night. She said that once she gave up caffeine, it was easy. She was never tired. Edna was always dressed, with her hair done up in a neat French twist and wearing her favorite pearl earrings, and she thrived on the little fifteen-minute catnaps she took on the couch whenever she felt like it.

Edna had lots of what at first seemed to Bunny to be crackpot ideas about health, but the more Edna explained them, the more sense they made. They were theories developed by Joyce, Edna's late partner, who'd been a pioneer in holistic medicine. Joyce believed that most disease was caused by a pH imbalance and that the only medicines a person needed were Milk of Magnesia and organic apple cider vinegar. Diseases, according to Joyce, could be characterized as acidic or alkaline. Most viruses were acidic and responded to an alkaline treatment. Reach for the blue bottle. Most cancers were alkaline and could be treated with the vinegar cruet elixir.

That's how Edna doctored herself, and except for her macular degeneration, which was an age-related deterioration that Edna managed with an enormous magnifying glass, she was in perfect health. She believed in the dispersion as opposed to the aggregation of calories—it was best to eat ten small meals of one-hundred and twenty calories each than three large meals totaling twelve-hundred calories. She had a bounce to her step, a lilt to her voice. She avoided salt and sugar, shunned refined and processed food, and took a teaspoon of raw honey every morning and two activated charcoal tablets in the evening. Crisco was her night cream, and any and all wounds or skin abrasions were doctored with a mysterious black salve that looked and smelled like tar and was kept in a jelly jar. Edna exercised her mind (Nintendo) and her body ("Sweatin' to the Oldies") and maintained a positive outlook on life. She laughed a lot.

And so, during those hours with Edna, Bunny laughed, too.

It was only a few months after coming across Connie's obituary that the letter arrived, postmarked from Palm Springs and addressed to Bunny in Gerald's still recognizable left-handed penmanship. It was a thick, business-size envelope, and Bunny let it sit on the kitchen counter all afternoon and evening. She got up twice during the night and looked at it, handled it, then put it back on the counter. She couldn't sleep. She thought of burning the letter or writing RETURN TO SENDER in thick block printing across the address and slipping it back in the mailbox. But she didn't. She let it season there on the counter through the night, like sauerbraten.

The next morning, after lopping the kudzu, she took the letter over to Edna's.

"I knew it," Edna said. "Well, let's hear what the old goat has to say."

Bunny sliced open the envelope with Edna's hammered-copper letter opener.

"Dear Bunny," the letter began. It was a long letter on lined notebook paper. Unapologetically, Gerald said he was grieving for Connie, who had died a slow, horrible death from cancer, but that his grief, too, had deeper roots. He was grieving now for his own life and the pain he had caused Bunny, for his infidelity, and the horrible mess he had created. The children—Ansel and Agnes—had never accepted him. They were estranged and angry, and his and Connie's marriage had never been what they had hoped it would be. There was always the dark cloud of resentment and regret looming over them. An indiscretion turned into a nightmare. He'd never even set eyes on his grandchildren, he said. (*Boo-hoo-hoo*, Bunny thought, reading that line.) And now, retired and widowed, he was sorry for so many things he'd done. He wanted to make peace—with his children and with Bunny—before he himself died. (*So he's in A.A.*, Bunny thought.) Gerald begged Bunny not for forgiveness but only for acknowledgment of his sincere contrition. Would she send some word? Something to let him know that she had read his letter, heard him out?

As a P.S., Gerald added that he was sorry that she was "stuck" with the geodesic dome she'd never liked and that in spite of the structure's many failings, he still thought fondly of the time when they'd built it and how, in their youth, they had whole-heartedly embraced a dream that cast off the old, rigid constructs of the past and held the gleaming hope of the future. The dome, he said, was the embodiment of all that: iconoclastic, innovative, inspired, totemic of the times. Even if it did leak.

And as a P.P.S., he mentioned that he had heard in a roundabout way of Bunny's brother's—Jack's—death, and that he was truly sorry. He knew how much Bunny admired and looked up to Jack, he said, and he always thought of Jack as a good man, a true "man of the cloth," even though he'd only met him once, briefly.

With the letter's mention of Jack, Bunny began to feel a panic attack coming on. Her voice wavered as she read those lines. Jack was ten years older than she, and as a child, Bunny adored him. He went away to boarding school when Bunny was only six, and then on to seminary, and then, when Bunny was just a teenager, Jack was ordained. He was a priest—a missionary—and she only saw him a few times after that, tall and handsome in his dark vestments and stiff white collar.

When Bunny was in kindergarten, Jack walked her home from school and babysat her until their mother got home from her job as a bank teller. All her life, Bunny had idolized Jack, and often she dreamed of him, sometimes strange, erotic dreams that made her ashamed, embarrassed, and confused. In her dresser drawer, she had a photograph of herself and Jack, when she was just a baby. In the photo, Jack was a little boy—probably eleven—in short pants and argyle knee socks and a white shirt with a Peter Pan collar and a little crooked clip-on bowtie. A heavily tinseled Christmas tree loomed in the background, and Jack sat on the overstuffed couch, holding Bunny on his lap, beaming at the camera. On the back, in ballpoint pen, her mother had written: JACK, JR. AND BRENDA, CHRISTMAS 1951. The ink had bled through the paper and left its mark across the front of the photo. It was Jack who gave her the nickname Bunny.

It was shortly after Jack's death that Bunny's mother called her. She was in her late eighties then, had been widowed for many years, and her heart was bad. She called Bunny from the hospital after a heart attack, the last phone call she would ever make, as far as Bunny knew. Her mother's voice was weak and shaky.

"Bunny," she said. "I'm dying, and there's something I have to say to you. Something I've kept buried inside me for forty-seven years."

Bunny couldn't speak.

"Bunny," her mother went on. "I know what Jack did to you. I came home early one day and found the both of you . . . and at the time," her mother went on, "at the time, I thought the best thing to do was not to ever mention it again to you and that, in time, you'd forget. I knew if I told your father, he'd have killed Jack. He would have killed him, Bunny. I know that for certain. And then your father would have gone to prison. And then you'd have been without a brother *and* a father, and I'd have been without a husband . . . . What would we have done, Bunny? What else could I do?"

There was a long pause. Bunny could hear her mother sobbing, but she still couldn't speak. "Bunny," she said, "I sent Jack away, and I told him he would have to enter the priesthood to pay for his crime, or I'd tell his father. . . Bunny, your father would have killed him."

Bunny's mind was racing. Remembering . . . remembering what? She still couldn't speak.

"But, Bunny," her mother said, "Jack paid. Jack paid with his life. He never wanted to be a priest. Please find it in your heart to forgive him. Now that he's dead. Forgive him. And, please, Bunny . . . Bunny, please, forgive me, too. I only did what I thought was best."

And then her mother hung up.

And then she died.

And Bunny had never said anything beyond *Hello* when she answered the phone.

Oddly enough, it might seem to some, Bunny's mother's confession did not arouse in Bunny a hatred of Jack. What it did was make her angry at her mother for unloading this information on her. Bunny's mother knew that she adored Jack. If that adoration had involved something taboo, however illicit the act, it was still committed out of love and innocence. Jack was a boy then, a boy of fourteen or fifteen. His frontal lobes weren't fully developed yet. Children, we like to imagine, are not sexual beings. Oh, but they are. Bunny's mother should have kept her mouth shut and taken her secret, like her bones, to her grave.

Bunny was confused and angry. Why had her mother told her

this? The dreams about Jack . . . now they made sense. The frigidity. But now that they made sense, were things worse or better? Did she need to know this?

No. She'd been better off with the ignorance, she thought. Still, she could never again look at the cherished snapshot of herself and Jack.

Years ago, her mother had done the right thing with respect to Bunny: never mentioning it again. But what about Jack? Bunny hadn't known that what she and Jack had done was wrong, and she had forgotten all about it. Resurrecting it was a horrid thing to do, her mother cleansing her own conscience before she died, but in doing so, passing onto Bunny a terrible, sickly knowledge that now *she* would have to live with until she died.

She didn't want to know.

"Well . . ." Edna said. She didn't notice Bunny's hands shaking as she folded the letter. "What do you make of it?"

"I don't know," Bunny managed. "I just don't know."

"Well," Edna continued. "I do. *Carpe diem*, my dear. The power is yours. He has given you the power to absolve him—or, as he put it, "acknowledge the wrong he's done"—the same thing, I'm sure—and you, my dear, can be magnanimous and grant him that atonement, or you can punish him and deny it. It's all up to you."

"What would you do?" Bunny asked.

"It doesn't matter what I'd do," Edna replied.

Bunny took the letter home and hid it behind the toaster, then she moved it to a desk drawer, and then into the china cabinet, folded into a soup tureen with a lid, but wherever she put it, it called to her. *Bunny,* the letter whispered, *Bunny, please.* She couldn't ignore it. Later that night, she opened her bureau drawer and took out the picture of herself and Jack and stared at it for a long time.

What good did it do to dwell on the past? What good was anger? And really, at some level and to some degree, wasn't everybody angry—just a little bit angry, at the least—about all the things denied them, all the disappointments in life, everything they deserved but didn't get and somebody else got instead: money, recognition, love? About everything they've lost: youth, good looks, love, innocence, husbands, friends. About all the insults to the body, insults to the mind, the ceaseless heartbreak of living. Angry about the inequities inherent in the world, environmental degradation, greed and poverty and war. Angry about stupid and ruthless leaders, the economic crisis, cruelty to animals, man's inhumanity to man, the academic theater of dunces, and most of all, angry about death itself. Angry at their own inability to control their anger. Really, everyone was in the same boat. It was like looking at one of those Where's Waldo pictures—only if you looked long enough and hard enough you'd find yourself, along with everybody you knew, along with everybody in the whole world, angry but smiling, smiling, smiling, in the great sea of faces.

She decided to write to Gerald. She took out a blank notecard. "So sorry about Connie," she wrote. "In an ideal world, things would have turned out better for all of us. Sincerely, Bunny." And then as a P.S., she added, "I have actually come to like the dome and have made many improvements, mostly landscaping." She lifted the pen, and then after a moment added, "No hard feelings."

Quickly, she sealed the envelope and peeled off a stamp, retrieved Gerald's letter from underneath the television, copied the return address, and put the letter in her mailbox, flag up.

The next night, past midnight, a ruckus started up again across the street at the Cassuccio house. It was a Thursday, a balmy August night with a big bright moon as luminescent as a halogen security light.

At the third outburst of *Fuck you! Fuck you! Fuck you!*, instead of calling the police, Bunny got out of bed and dressed quickly.

In its original box, on a shelf in the back of the utility closet, Bunny had stashed a high-powered mini megaphone that she'd used to simulate the roar of a lion in an amateur production of *A Midsummer Night's Dream* she'd directed years ago. She dug it out and from the kitchen junk drawer, unearthed a package of AA batteries. She held the megaphone to her mouth and gave a little practice roar. Puck and Peaseblossom, who had been yinning and yanging around her ankles, skedaddled. Bunny picked up the megaphone and stepped outside. She stomped over to Edna's and gave her signature knock: Tap-Tap (pause) Tap-Tap-Tap-Tap.

Edna answered the door, and Bunny laid out her plan.

Together then, they stood, obscured behind a wall of kudzu that had once been a privet hedge bordering Edna's front yard.

They waited.

The *Fuck you! Fuck you!* started up again.

Bunny lifted the megaphone, lowered her voice and let fly a loud *RRRRRROOOAAARRRR*, worthy of any Simba.

Edna giggled.

Silence.

RRRRRROOOAAARRRR!

Silence.

Then a male voice, *Fuck you!*

Yeah, fuck you! another male voice joined in.

"Die and be damned, you toad-suckled dewberry!" Bunny shouted through the megaphone.

Edna started to laugh, louder this time. "Give it to 'em," she egged Bunny on. "Give 'em hell, Bunny," Edna encouraged in a loud whisper, slapping Bunny on the back.

"A plague of boils and flies, you pigeon-livered, swag-bellied, puke-faced hedge-pigs!" Bunny shouted through the megaphone then doubled over with laughter, Edna in stitches beside her.

And then it came, not what they'd expected: A big voice—a big, lusty, sonorous, drunken baritone—an exaggerated cockney accent—fulminating from the Cassuccio's porch: "A pox on your house, you yeasty, rump-fed maggot-pies!"

And then laughter. Cheers and hooting and howling and uproarious laughter. Big booming bursts of crazy ping-ponging glorious laughter, bouncing back and forth across the kudzued street, tickling the night.

✦ A Forever Home ✦

"Oh, Sean, look at this one!" the girl cooed. "Just look at him, Sean. Look how tiny and old he is. He looks like a little old man. Ohmygawd, he's *sooooo* cute," she cooed again. "Poor, dear little thing. We could call him Rumplestiltskin or Uncle Wiggily or Mr. Peanut or Jiminy Cricket."

The girl had long, matted hair the color of chicken gravy, twisted into wooly dreadlocks and gathered up into a squirrel's nest on top of her head. She wore combat boots and pilled tights and a little fuzzy pink rag of a skirt no bigger than a hand towel, an old Harley Davidson motorcycle jacket many sizes too big, and huge round glasses. Sparkly rhinestones riveted the auricle of her left ear like a bejeweled bass clef. From her right ear, many tiny gold bells jingled.

"Cora," the young man said sternly. "No! Come on! We agreed to get a puppy. Not some decrepit old thing on its last legs. You said you wanted a puppy. That's what we agreed on."

The boy, too, had dreadlocks, but his were stuffed into an oversized knit cap that made his head cast a shadow like an enormous light bulb. His pants hung low on his hips, cinched by a wide, studded belt. Plaid boxer shorts poofed out above what was supposed to be the waistband of the pants.

"But, Sean, just look at him. We can't just leave him here. He looks so sad. He's *sooooo* dear."

"Corrrrrrrrrrrr-a!" the young man sighed, exasperated. He hiked up his pants and jutted out a hip to give gravity something to think about. He grabbed the girl by the arm and pulled her around the corner and down another cinderblock and cement corridor lined with steel kennels stacked three high.

Everyone was barking and whining and meowing. It hurt Ponce de León's ears. He huddled in the back of his crate and put his head under his blankey. He wished he could go home. He liked the girl with the big glasses and pierced ears. He liked her voice, which had a little squeak to it like Nina's, but he was afraid. Earlier that day, someone had taken his picture, nearly blinding him with the flash, and someone else had written his bio in a stupid persona that was supposed to be him talking.

"*Arf! Arf!*" his bio said. "Aren't I cute? My name is Ponce de León, and I'm an 18-pound, male wire-haired fox terrier. I am around nine years old, and I am very smart, affectionate, and gentle. It goes without saying that I am housebroken and well-behaved. I was found sleeping at the foot of the Gibson-Brown angel in East Oak Grove Cemetery. I was very tired and lonely and hungry. I whimpered and rolled over on my back, exposing my tender belly, when the Animal Friends volunteer approached me, and I raised my paw politely when offered a pepperoni treat. My mistress has died, and I ran away from home. I am very healthy. All my medical records are on file at Paw Prints Veterinary Clinic where I have visited regularly for the past eight years. At Paw Prints, they all know me and love me because I am such a charming, good boy. One time I won a Halloween contest at Mountaineer Mall, dressed as the Lone Ranger. Please make me yours and give me a forever home. *Arf! Arf!*"

It was so embarrassing, that Pet-of-the-Week dog voice. And this was not Ponce de León's first encounter with THE VOICE. He'd been here before, in fact, in the very same shelter—eight years ago, but he really couldn't complain. THE VOICE (and a similar photo) had brought Nina to his rescue that time.

"Here," the boy said. "This one." He was squatting in front of a little black Lab-ish puppy with paws the size of MoonPies. The inside of the puppy's crate was a mass of shredded fabric and globs of polyester stuffing, the remains of a dog bed and numerous eviscerated toys.

"Just look at him!" the boy said, sticking his hand sideways between the bars of the crate. The puppy licked and gnawed at the boy's fingers and wagged its tail full circle like a propeller.

"Just look at him!" the boy said again. Gravity had won the pants contest. The pants now appeared as a sling, the red plaid boxer shorts in full view. The girl, however, was nowhere in sight.

Out in the car—a rusty 1989 Subaru sedan—the girl tried to hold on to the squirming puppy, who had already managed to turn on the hazard lights, chew the knob off of the gear shifter, swallow one of her bell earrings, and piddle on her skirt while the boy drove down the windy dirt road from the Animal Friends shelter. Ponce de León hunkered down between the girl's combat boots, half under the seat, shaking.

He would have preferred the back seat where he could see out, but that was taken up by a cat carrier with two cats—Helvetica and Times—who had been living for years outside an old print shop along the railroad tracks. The print shop had been demolished to make way for an urban renewal project that included townhouses, shops, restaurants, and a theater. Not cats. Somehow, Helvetica and Times had found their way out of the Animal Friends shelter and into the boy and girl's car, too.

Truth was, Helvetica was relieved to have been caught and spayed. She'd had more litters than she could count, and she didn't even enjoy her estrus anymore. She'd been faking her cat call for years and was looking forward to retirement as a pampered indoor cat, sleeping in a sunny, southern exposure window, birdwatching out of one eye; eating tasty Nine Lives tuna day in and day out; batting about a catnip mouse every now and then to entertain the humans, or, on special occasions when company was present, making a spectacular, Nureyev-worthy leap at a stupid feather dangling on a strand of elastic suspended from a doorjamb.

Times, however, was livid about the neutering. He'd put up a struggle when he was trapped and tore right through the animal control officer's gloves, inciting a case of cat-scratch fever that had hospitalized the officer for three days. Times would never give up fighting and catting around, balls or no. Even in the shelter, he sprayed ceaselessly and strutted about their cage, proudly displaying his left profile, which showcased a cauliflower ear bitten down to a lumpy stub by a manx. Times had won that fight, though, paws down; he'd put out the manx's eye.

All four Animal Friends adoptees were absolutely free and came with dry and tinned food, flea medicine, treats and catnip, all of which had been donated to the shelter, and they had health certificates verifying that their vaccinations were up to date, and all Cora and Sean had to do was sign adoption contracts saying that if they could not keep any of their new pets—for any reason—they promised to return them, no questions asked, to the Animal Friends shelter.

Moose—what Sean named the black Lab-Great Dane-mix puppy—was exuberant to be adopted; Ponce de León was nervous and apprehensive; and Helvetica and Times were not entirely pleased—to put it mildly—with the adoption arrangements. Helvetica would have preferred a canine-free environment, but she agreed with Times that the puppy was no challenge whatsoever: a few swats on the nose, maybe a little bull ride on its back, and they'd have it under control. "Besides," Helvetica pointed out, "Labs are more interested in the litter box than the cat."

Times was angry about the whole situation and disgruntled about the prospect of living with a terrier. His ideal situation would have been barn cat. Lord of the Cows, rat catcher, snake charmer.

"They're full of piss and vinegar," he said, referring to Ponce de León's breed. "Crafty little demons," he said, spraying the back seat of the Subaru through the mesh window of the cat carrier. "And stubborn. They never back down or give up a fight."

"Yeah, but look how old and feeble he is," Helvetica consoled him. "Piece o' cake. Besides," she added, raising a back leg behind her head and licking her butt, "I thought you said you were going to run away as soon as they opened the door."

Which he did.

The Subaru rattled down River Road and then down another dirt road, this one with potholes the size of washtubs. The descent was steep. Cora and Sean lived outside of town, along the river and the railroad tracks, in a mobile home on a remote, abandoned homestead designated in the property tax books in the Monongalia County courthouse as Lock Eleven, but most people called the place the Drowned Man's House.

The job of lockmaster had once been a respected position, one held by a civil engineer, a member of the U.S. Army Corps of Engineers. Lockmasters were responsible for overseeing the maintenance of the locks and dams, which controlled flooding and ensured year-round navigation on the Monongahela River. The lockmasters' houses had been built by the Corps with no expenses barred, meant to serve as an attractive compensation for the lockmasters and their families who had to live outside the city limits, along the river and the railroad tracks.

The house at Lock Eleven was built and first occupied in 1902. It was a grand, sprawling Victorian the pale yellow of French vanilla ice cream, with maroon and spruce trim, and with all the standard Painted Lady features and embellishments: turrets and gables, gingerbread and transoms and stained glass, front and back staircases, and a big sweep of a wraparound porch that entertained the breeze from the river. Six slender and ornate yellow brick chimneys decorated the slate roof, and a stand of cottonwoods marched down the lush lawn to the cement dock. "The Cottonwoods," the house at Lock Eleven was once called.

At the turn of the twentieth century and up until mid-century, The Cottonwoods was a showpiece along the river, a landmark known to rail and riverboat travelers alike, something to be pointed to and admired. But in the forties, the original stone and timber locks of Lock Eleven were beginning to fail, and construction on a large, comprehensive lock and dam system that would eliminate many of the original locks, including Lock Eleven, was begun. That Army Corps of Engineers project was completed in 1950.

The original lockmaster was a man named Homer Martin, who came to live at The Cottonwoods when he was a young civil engineer. After the demise of Lock Eleven, he remained in the house alone for many years. His children were grown—there had been many—and they'd moved away, and his wife had died on April 12, 1945, the same day as FDR. Homer Martin was an old man in 1956, when down on his dock, puttering about, he spotted a woman and a child in a rowboat about twenty feet from shore. He waved. The woman was rowing, and the child was dipping a can into the river, ladling up water and pouring it back. Suddenly, the child toppled over the side of the boat, and the woman sitting in the stern began to scream and the boat began to rock. Homer Martin kicked off his shoes and dove off the dock and swam out and dove down again and again and saved the child. He grabbed her by her hair. Homer Martin was still a strong swimmer in spite of his years, but as he handed the small girl up to the woman in the boat, the old lockmaster's heart gave out, and he went under one last time.

A large grapevine wreath hung on the dock of Lock Eleven for many years, but rather rapidly, the house fell into disrepair. First came the teenagers, carloads of them, driving down the dirt road in their Chevys and DeSotos with their Pabst Blue Ribbon bottles and Lucky Strike cigarettes, and behind them came the thieves and pillagers with their crowbars, and years later, the vandals with their cans of spray paint. The windows of the Drowned Man's House—as The Cottonwoods then came to be known—were broken, and the stained glass stolen, as well as the leaded glass built-ins, the crown moldings, the newel post and banisters, the chandeliers, the doors, the oak floorboards. But because what was left of the house at Lock Eleven was easily accessible from the railroad tracks, yet remote and difficult to reach by land, the road having not been kept up, The Cottonwoods became a shelter for drifters, and a homeless camp grew up around it, and eventually the clapboards were ripped off the house and fed to bonfires, and then went the lathing strips and studs. Broken bottles and sardine and tuna fish tins and cigarette butts and syringes and cardboard Tampax tubes and condoms littered the grounds. In no time, there was just a pile of slate roof tiles and the foundation: a fieldstone grave, home to snakes and spiders, vermin and such.

The twenty-three-acre stretch of property along the railroad tracks known as Lock Eleven was sold at public auction in 1985, because Uncle Sam wanted to offload the liability. The developer who bought The Cottonwoods was Cora's father. Cora was just a baby then. Now her father was happy to have her out of his house, living out at The Cottonwoods—Cora and her dreadlocks and piercings and tattoos.

When the rusty Subaru turned off the River Road and began the steep, winding descent down the crumbling road to Lock Eleven, Cora rolled down the window, and Ponce de León could smell the river and the river mud and the staghorn sumacs and the onion grass and wild carrot and the road dust tainted with creosote from old railroad ties, and the lingering smell of campfires and burnt garbage and piss.

Ponce de León pricked his ears and sat up between Cora's boots. He'd been here before.

It was many years ago. Another life. A life before Nina, a life with Prophet Zero in the homeless camp.

Ponce de León jumped out of the car and sniffed about, Moose bounding after him. They went down to the river's edge near the old iron bridge where Ponce de León had often seen the ghost of Homer Martin walking about at night in the shadows of the cottonwood trees. Sometimes he saw Homer Martin sitting on the big cornerstone of the old foundation. He smelled like sweet cherry pipe tobacco. Some of the drifters who camped at The Cottonwoods nearby had seen the old lockmaster, too, and they were frightened of him, but Ponce de León knew there was no reason to fear ghosts and that the ghost of Homer Martin lingered only because he was not ready to leave this place he had loved and cared for so well. Homer Martin still longed for earthly things, the sounds and smells of the river and the land: the toll of the tugboat bells and the moan of the barges and the music of the freight trains and the first jack-in-the-pulpits and Dutchman's breeches peeping out from under the dead leaves in the woodlands come spring. And after Prophet Zero died, Ponce de León saw him, too, sitting with the old lockmaster, watching the trains, and sometimes Ponce de León sat with them. He, too, loved the river and the barges and the trains.

Moose jumped in the river and paddled about, and Ponce de León scampered down the railroad tracks toward the hobo camp, hoping to see his old pals, Angel and Car Wash and Q-Tip. But when Ponce de León came to where the camp used to be, there was no one there. The area was closed off with a high chain-link fence along the bank as far as Ponce de León could see, and warning signs on stout posts had been erected. KEEP OUT, the signs said. PRIVATE PROPERTY. NO TRESPASSING.

NO CAMPING. TRESPASSERS WILL BE PROSECUTED. — Lock 11-Cottonwoods Upgrade, Phase I, WV Permit #W7682-B-26501.

Ponce de León was happy living with Cora and Sean and Moose and Helvetica at Lock Eleven. Soon it was summer, and Ponce de León spent most of the day in the garden with Cora. Moose was not allowed in the garden because he was unruly and dug things up as fast as Cora planted them. Moose was big now and clumsy. "Goofy," Cora called him.

The days were long and the ground was warm, and Ponce de León spent many hours exploring, walking along the railroad tracks toward town, the way he used to walk with Prophet Zero. Moose had to be tied up most of the time because he ran off and he chased deer and one time had dragged home the carcass of a fawn. He rolled in mud and anything putrid or dead, too. "Mudpie," Cora sometimes called him, too, or just plain "Stinky."

Early on Saturday mornings, Cora and Sean and Ponce de León drove into the town square and set up a table at the farmer's market where they sold vegetables and flowers and ground-cherry jam.

The evenings were cool and sprinkled with lightning bugs and meteor showers. Ponce de León slept at the bottom of the bed on Cora's side, just how he used to sleep with Nina. Sometimes Helvetica slept there, too. Moose had to sleep on the back porch because he was so big and so stinky. Times had fallen in with a band of feral cats, kittens that had been dumped off on the River Road and left to fend for themselves. Sometimes, late at night, Helvetica heard him screaming outside the bedroom window. "*Old love,*" she hummed to herself, "*leave me alone,*" and rolled over.

Fall came and brought wind and leaf rain, chevrons of honking geese in the sky, bonfires, and a great production of canning salsa in the kitchen.

"Old Man," the boy called Ponce de León. "Old Man" or "Methuselah."

"How goes it, Methuselah?" the boy would say to Ponce de León each morning as he sat in one of the captain's chairs lacing up his Doc Martens. The boy was a tattoo artist at Wild Ink, and the girl—Cora—was his canvas. Ponce de León was amazed and intrigued by the pictures and text on Cora's body: Popeye the Sailor Man with a can of spinach on one bicep; a smiling Sarah Palin with the inscription I CAN SEE RUSSIA FROM MY HOUSE on the other; Edgar Allen Poe with a raven on his head on one forearm.

Staring out from the back of Cora's neck was a small eye in a triangle, like the one forming the tip of the pyramid on the Great Seal, underneath it the motto, *Novus Ordo Seclorum*. A colorfully illustrated map of the Appalachian Trail decorated Cora's back, from Georgia on her left hip to Maine on her right shoulder, complete with representative flora and fauna: a Wake Robin trillium, a serviceberry tree, a porcupine, a moose, a copperhead, a bald eagle. The seven deadly sins formed a bracelet on her right wrist: LUST, GLUTTONY, WRATH, ENVY, PRIDE, SLOTH, GREED; a Salvador Dali clock melted around her left wrist. The seven heavenly virtues—FAITH, HOPE, CHARITY, PRUDENCE, JUSTICE, TEMPERANCE, and COURAGE—encircled her right ankle, while the opening lines of "Deteriorata" adorned her chest, and the Beatitudes in lovely Zapfino script traversed the outside of her right thigh and calf. *Blessed are the poor . . . Blessed are the meek . . . Blessed are the merciful . . . Blessed are they who mourn for they shall be comforted . . .*

One afternoon Cora asked Ponce de León if he would like to go for a ride, go into town with her to visit a friend. Ponce de León scampered to the back door. It was not going to be a fun visit, Cora told him (she talked to him all the time, like he was a person, like Nina had talked to him), but it was something they had to do. They were in the Subaru, rattling into town. Ponce de León had given up barking at everything that moved. It was too much effort. Besides, it was futile; everything kept on moving, and nobody responded to his barking. Not like Steve, the mailman at Nina's, who always left the porch after a furious, successful barking reprimand to *Get away! Go! Go!*

They drove perhaps twenty minutes, up the dirt road from Lock Eleven, down the River Road, across the railroad tracks and over a bridge, down the boulevard and through many traffic lights and then across another bridge and into a neighborhood Ponce de León immediately recognized. It was his old home place—Chancery Hill—the neighborhood where he had lived most of his life with Nina before Nina died. He stuck his head out the window. He saw the funeral home and the car wash he had walked by every day, the brick house where the Scottie dog, Sweetie, lived, and the house up the street with the picket fence where the English cocker spaniel, Nellie, lived; and behind there, he knew, down the alley, Sally the mongrel was always up for a little fence fight. And farther down the alley lived Buddy the beagle/German shepherd mix, and Molly the standard poodle, and Missy the pomeranian and Bella Donna the toy Yorkie no bigger than a guinea pig. He watched everything go by. And then there was his house. The burning bushes were a fiery red. The catbird meowed from the yews.

Cora parked in the alley, and Ponce de León got out and sniffed about. Another dog had been there recently. A big dog.

"Come on, Cricket," Cora said. "This way." "Cricket," Cora called him most of the time, "My little Jiminy Cricket."

They went to the back door of the house directly across the alley from Nina's. A young woman with red-rimmed eyes and a puffy face let them in. Her name was Ramona, and she and Cora embraced.

"I'm so sorry, Ramona," Cora said. "I'm sorry I've not been in to see you. I've just been so busy with the garden and all—"

"Oh, Cora, I know. I know how it is. We have such different lives now that we're married. I've been meaning to bring Billy out to your place, too."

They went into the living room, which was dark and cluttered with books and toys. Reggae music was playing. Ramona dabbed at her eyes and blew her nose and thanked Cora for coming. "I know it will be okay," she said, and cried a little more. "It's just such a disappointment. But thank God we have Billy. There won't be any more children, the doctor said." And Ramona started to cry again.

No woman, no cry, Bob Marley was singing, *No woman, no cry.*

And Ramona cried some more.

Ponce de León hated it when people cried. He started to quiver, and Cora reached down and patted him. "It's okay, Little Man," she said. That's what Nina had called him, too, sometimes, "Little Man."

"He's so sensitive," Cora said to Ramona. "He's my little canine mood ring. Aren't you, Cricket?"

"The lady who used to live behind us had a little dog who looked a lot like him. I wonder what happened to him after she died," Ramona said. "Oh, he *is* cute, Cora. Maybe we'll get a dog like him for Billy when he's a little older," Ramona said and stroked Ponce de León's back.

"I love him, but I don't know whether we can keep him," Cora said and hesitated.

"Why?"

"We're thinking about traveling. Maybe to Australia and New Zealand. Maybe staying there. Sean says there are lots of opportunities in New Zealand. Land is cheap, and the economy is good. I don't know. I don't know whether I really want to leave. It's Sean. But I just can't leave Cricket."

Cora lit a cigarette, waiting.

"I asked Sean if we couldn't wait a couple of years," Cora continued. "I mean, Cricket is so old. He's not going to live that long."

"What did he say?" Ramona asked.

"He said you can't plan your life around a dog."

"I don't know," Ramona said. "I mean, you wouldn't abandon a child. It's the same commitment. I don't know. Is a dog any different?"

"I don't know," Cora said. "It's an ethical question. But just saying, 'Well, let's wait until Cricket dies' seems so . . . I don't know so . . . so . . . crass, somehow, so inhuman.

"I don't know either," Cora continued, "Sean says we can take Cricket and Helvetica back to the Animal Friends shelter, and someone else will give them a good home—it's a no-kill shelter—but it just doesn't seem right to me."

"What about the other dog, the big goofy one? What's his name?"

"Moose. Sean's friend Arlo says he'll take Moose. They live out in the country, too, and Moose is so happy and gregarious, he'd be happy anywhere, especially some place where he can run. And Helvetica. Well, she's no trouble at all. But it's just not the same with Cricket. Nobody wants an old dog."

"Well, it sounds like you're going. I mean, it sounds like Sean is making arrangements. You'll go with him, Cora, won't you? You're not thinking about splitting up, are you?" Ramona asked.

"But we made a commitment to them," Cora said, stroking Ponce de León's ears. "We promised them a forever home. You just can't abandon your animal friends because you want a different life and they don't fit in. I'm just afraid it might be a decision I'd regret for the rest of my life. And it makes me question the kind of person Sean really is. I mean . . . if he'd leave Moose and Cricket and Helvetica, would he leave me? We had a big fight about it."

"I'm sorry," Ramona said and took a drink from a tall, sweating glass.

Ponce de León heard every word Cora said, and he trembled. Lots of people think that dogs don't understand human languages, but they're wrong. Ponce de León understood English. English was easy. He lay by Cora's feet and pretended to be asleep, although he was still quivering. He didn't want to go back to the shelter. He loved Cora and her bells and tattoos. He'd only lived with her for seven months, but he loved her just like he'd loved Nina and before her, Prophet Zero. He would never leave Cora, no matter what opportunity came his way.

"An old dog can be a big expense," Ramona said. "I mean, veterinarians cost as much as, if not more than, people doctors, and of course, insurance doesn't cover dogs. And Noah has two more years of school and then his dissertation. I mean—"

Cora knew what Ramona was implying: they couldn't afford the financial burden of an old dog—and so she changed the subject.

As the young women talked, Ponce de León got up and stretched and explored the downstairs. That's what he was: an explorer. That's what Nina said. He was quite shaken by the conversation he'd overheard between Cora and Ramona, but he was also excited to be back in his old neighborhood. He'd seen the outside of Ramona's house many times from the kitchen window of Nina's house across the alley, but he'd never been inside. He remembered the woman Ramona pushing a baby stroller down the alley. Sometimes a young man with a ponytail and a slight limp walked beside her. Ponce de León had enjoyed barking at them.

When no one was looking, Ponce de León tiptoed up the stairs. He had a good sense of spatial relations, and he knew that from the back of this house, he'd be able to look out and see his old house, see his favorite barking spot in the kitchen window.

In a small bedroom at the top of the stairs, the shades were drawn and a musical mobile was playing, a carousel of painted ponies spinning. In a corner of the room, by the window, a little boy lay in a tiny bed with a short railing, clutching a blanket and sniffling.

The little boy sat up. "Dog," he said and laughed his little boy laugh.

Ponce de León jumped up on the bed. The little boy giggled and patted Ponce de León's head.

"Dog," the little boy Billy said again.

Ponce de León licked his face, and Billy squealed and petted him some more. From the bedroom window, Ponce de León could look down and see the kitchen window from where he used to watch for Nina. He felt strange and sad, looking at his old house and remembering his old life, himself looking out the window he was now looking in. In Nina's house, a different dog—a boxer—was looking out from his old favorite lookout. It was hard to comprehend, this boxer looking back at him from *his* spot. Ponce de León's life came rushing back to him. He remembered how he'd ridden in a boxcar with Prophet Zero and lived at The Cottonwoods and how he used to walk with Prophet Zero into town and wait outside the soup kitchens and how all the homeless people coddled him and the soup kitchen staff gave him scraps and bones and how Zero used to preach in front of Family Dollar and all the college kids knew them and made a fuss over Ponce de León, too. His name was Lucky then.

This is what Ponce de León knew: 1) at any minute, your life could change, even your name; 2) at any minute you could end up back where you started; 3) at any minute you might have to leave home; 4) at any minute, someone you loved might leave you.

Billy lay down and put his thumb in his mouth, one arm around Ponce de León, and fell asleep. Ponce de León closed his eyes. He slept, too, lightly, and he dreamed he saw Nina out in his old backyard by the burning bushes, hanging up laundry. He saw so clearly her kind face, and he remembered with sadness how sick and weak she had been and how just before she died, she looked like an angel to him. Here is another thing Ponce de León knew: the dead never really leave us.

Billy sighed in his sleep, and Ponce de León curled up against him. He liked it here with Billy in his little bed by the window with the view of his old house, but he loved Cora, too, and The Cottonwoods. He felt old and tired.

"Where's my little Cricket?" he heard Cora call. "Cricket!"

Cora was at the bottom of the stairs. Ponce de León knew that if he pretended to be asleep, she'd come upstairs and find him and tiptoe back down and get Ramona, and they'd both tiptoe back up and see him sleeping there with Billy, and his fate would be sealed. Cora would be free to go to New Zealand, and he would be Billy's dog. And then some day, he'd cross over and he'd be Nina's and Zero's dog again, too. And he'd see Cora again, too, sooner or later, in what Nina had called the Sweet Hereafter, and little Billy would meet him there, too, someday, he knew.

And if he ran down the stairs? Then Cora would have to choose between him and Sean and maybe Regret would follow her all the days of her life.

The catbird called again, *Meow, Meow,* from its nest deep inside the tangled branches of the overgrown yew, and as he had seen Asta the wire-haired fox terrier do in the old Thin Man movies that he and Nina had loved to watch again and again, Ponce de León covered his eyes with his paws and feigned sleep.

✦ Help Wanted: Female ✦

PART II

After her brief stint as a word processor, Wendy found it impossible to find a job. Of course, she didn't have a reference from BG&D. Who would she ask for a recommendation? The lecherous Bob Boldt? And there was a little problem with her resumé, which was beginning to look like it belonged to a migrant worker: two pages of hit-and-run encounters in the American workforce. Plus, the troublesome job application questions she was bound to encounter: *years* employed, contact person, reason for leaving.

In consultation with her best friend, Roger, *it was suggested that* the recent word processing job with the unhappy ending be eliminated from the resumé, but when Wendy pointed out that word processing was a very marketable skill and maybe the *only* marketable skill she possessed, *it was decided* by all those present that the name BG&D should be changed and the dates of employment be slightly altered to embrace a more reasonable chunk of time—two or three years, perhaps, rather than the actual six weeks.

It was also decided—by a unanimous vote—that Roger, along with his phone number, be listed as the reference/contact and that Wendy's most recent employment should have been with a private law firm of which Roger was senior counsel, and that Wendy's duties—in addition to word processing—should be slightly expanded to include the preparation of briefs, the maintenance of the law library, and recommendations to the law partners concerning the best solutions for resolving and presenting cases.

Some of these job responsibilities Roger had found under the heading "paralegal" in a library book entitled *What Color Is Your Parachute?*, a title that suggested to Wendy a sky full of Blondie and Dagwood Bumsteads in navy blue suits, dropping like marines onto Normandy Beach, then racing down city sidewalks, swinging briefcases and umbrellas, and sporting big shit-eating grins.

This minor change in the word processing job description and dates solved many of the resumé and potential application problems and also provided the incentive for the elaboration and enhancement of other job titles, responsibilities, and dates of employment, which, in turn, required only the slightest transposition of contact phone numbers—a boo-boo that even the most careful person might make.

On paper, Wendy looked damn good. Proofreading the new resumé, which Roger had meticulously typed, she felt confident. And in her Mary Tyler Moore wig, which expertly concealed her spiked and parti-colored hair; her über-conservative Liz Claiborne suit; her sensible Naturalizer shoes with the half-inch stacked heels; and her slightly scuffed Etienne Aigner briefcase—all scored for next-to-nothing on a double discount Tuesday at Volunteers of America—Wendy was ready to re-enter the American workforce.

A month passed. No jobs.

At the unemployment office, the job counselor told Wendy that she was overqualified for the positions available. It was the master's degree in English literature that was holding her back, Mrs. Stradenko said. Mrs. Stradenko had a habit of tugging on one of her earlobes and smiling at the end of every sentence, as if her ear was the trigger of some mechanical device that dispatched end-punctuation like pellets for a trained rat, and the smile was some rudimentary brain stem-elicited expression of satisfaction, like the smile of a baby passing gas. Mrs. Stradenko's bright orange-ish eyebrows were so exaggerated and thickly drawn that they reminded Wendy of the McDonald's arches. All of Mrs. Stradenko's makeup, in fact, was so boldly and crudely applied that she looked like a finger painting of herself.

It was late afternoon, and the heat in the windowless unemployment office had gone kafooey. The temperature had become tropical, Mrs. Stradenko's cubicle a tanning bed. Everyone was sweating, and Mrs. Stradenko's makeup had begun to melt. Poor thing, she could have passed for Dirk Bogarde playing Gustav von Aschenbach in the last scene of *Death in Venice*.

Back home, Wendy took scissors to the master copy of the perfectly typed resumé and extracted the master's degree in English literature under Education. Carefully then, she sliced between all the entries under Job History and then rubber cemented all the sections back together on a clean sheet of typing paper, adding space between the entries to balance the page. It was an arduous task, especially for a butterfingers like Wendy, and the resulting document, even after careful feathering with White-Out and repeated Xeroxing at Kinko's, looked like a ransom note.

But it worked.

Two days later, Wendy spotted a brand new advertisement in the Help Wanted section of the *Dominion Post*:

HELP WANTED: DELIVERY PERSON. FLOWERS FROM COLOMBIA. MUST HAVE OWN CAR. APPLY IN PERSON BETWEEN 3:00 AND 4:00 P.M., FRIDAY, OCT. 2, ROOM 313, MONONGALIA BUILDING, HIGH STREET.

At the Monongalia Building—the most decrepit building downtown—a long line of desperate-looking people leaned against the wall approaching Room 313, which had a frosted glass window with a piece of notebook paper Scotch-taped to it, announcing in a sloppy ball-point cursive: "Flowers from Colombia. Apply here." The interviews were brief, with people leaving the room after only a minute or so, shaking their heads.

Wendy was next. The room was tiny—no bigger than a cell, really—and totally empty except for a man wearing black sweat pants, a black hoodie, and a black leather jacket, sporting shades and smoking a Kool. Wendy handed him her resumé.

"This your current address and phone number?" he asked.

"Yes, sir," Wendy answered, smiling. He folded the resume and put it in his pocket.

"Gimme your driver's license."

Wendy produced her driver's license, which the man studied, looking back and forth between the license and Wendy and seeming to study her hair for too long before handing the photo I.D. back.

"What kind of car do you drive?" he asked, and Wendy told him of the late-model Plymouth Horizon she'd recently inherited from her grandmother.

"Good. Do you live alone?" the man asked.

"Yes," Wendy answered, smiling.

"Good," he said. "Close the door."

Wendy closed the door.

"Here's what you do," he said. "Don't write anything down. Listen carefully, and then repeat these instructions back to me."

"Okay," Wendy said, smiling.

"At 9:00 p.m. tonight be at Hart Field. Don't take anybody with you, and don't tell anybody where you're going. At Hart Field, take the service road and park behind hangar #14. Turn off your lights and cut the engine. A yellow Cessna will land on the field and the pilot will deplane and walk through the gate. He will approach your car and ask you your name. Say, 'My name is Candy.' *Do not say anything else.* The pilot will return to the plane and begin to unload boxes. There will be seven boxes about yea big." He held his arms out to indicate the length of a box that maybe something like gladiolus or sunflowers or rifles might come in.

"Open the trunk of your car. Count them. Count the boxes. Seven. When all the boxes have been loaded, give the man this envelope. Lock the trunk and drive away."

A crow that had alighted on the windowsill behind the man gave Wendy a funny look and did a nosedive off its perch.

The interviewer reached into the inside pocket of his jacket and pulled out a sealed manila envelope and handed it to Wendy. The envelope was thick and weighty.

"*Do not open the envelope,*" he went on. "Put it in your briefcase now."

Using her knee as a prop, Wendy quickly snapped open her newly acquired briefcase and dropped the envelope inside, hoping the man wouldn't notice that the briefcase was empty except for a pack of Merit Ultralight 100s.

"Good. Now, got that?" the man asked. "Repeat it back to me."

Wendy repeated the instructions.

"Good. Good. Now the drop."

"The *what?*" Wendy asked.

"The delivery."

"Oh, yes, the flowers. Where do I deliver the flowers?"

"As you leave Hart Field, turn left onto Hartman Run Road. Drive to the traffic light in Sabraton and turn left onto Route 7 South. Drive 13 miles, through Dellslow, Cascade, and Brentz. At the four-way stop in Masontown, turn left onto Route 26 East, and in 2.2 miles you'll see a purple cement building with a neon sign that says ANGIE'S GOOD TIME and a gravel parking lot."

Wendy's head was spinning.

"Drive around to the back of the building," the man continued, "and honk your horn. A man will come out and ask your name."

"Candy," Wendy said.

"That's right, Candy. Good. Say, 'My name is Candy. Who are you?'"

"My name is Candy. Who are you?" Wendy repeated in her confident voice.

"Not now!" the man in black snapped.

"The man will say, 'My name is Groucho,'" the man in the leather jacket continued. "If he doesn't identify himself as Groucho—if he says any other name—drive away. Drive back to the strip mall on Route 7 in Masontown and park in back of the 24-Hour No. 1 Happy All-You-Can-Eat Chinese Buffet. Make sure that no one has followed you. Get out. Lock your car. Go inside and ask to use the phone. Dial this number: 344-499-5618. Don't write it down. 344-499-5618. Got that? Don't write anything down. Let the phone ring twice and then hang up. Sit in the first booth with your back to the door and wait for further instructions."

Phew. Wendy was getting really nervous. She tried to keep smiling, but her lips were vibrating like a Jew's harp, her heart was a Mexican jumping bean, her hands one of those perpetual motion gadgets, her legs

Velveeta cheese. She thought maybe she should run out, but the man had already divulged vital information. He might block her exit and slit her throat with a stiletto or shoot her in the back with a handgun equipped with a silencer or jab some kind of poison dart into her neck, paralyzing her while muffling her scream with his big hand and then throwing her out the window. She tried to pay attention, to memorize his face so she could identify him in a line-up, all the while trying to commit to memory everything the man in black told her.

"Repeat what I just told you," the man said.

Wendy got it right. "But what if it *is* Groucho?" she asked.

"Good. Now the man named Groucho will hand you an envelope. Open up the envelope and count the money. There should be one-hundred $500 bills. Count them. Count them in tens. Count them twice. If it's all there, unlock the trunk of your car and let the man named Groucho remove the boxes.

"Keep one of the $500 bills and put the rest of the money in this bag."

Wow! $500! Wendy registered. *Rent, plus utilities, plus car insurance, plus dog food, ramen noodles, tampons, gas, alcohol, and cigarettes for a month!* Wendy'd never even seen a $500 bill.

The man reached again inside his jacket and produced a zippered moneybag with a lock and key. "Lock the bag and drive away. Don't stop anywhere. Don't talk to anybody. Drive back here to Morgantown, directly to the First National Bank on the corner of High and Pleasant. Park your car. Make sure no one is watching. Get out and deposit the moneybag in the night depository box and drive away."

"Uhm. But what about the key?" Wendy asked.

"Swallow it," the man said, laughing, then added, "and remember, Wendy, I know where you live." He grinned and patted his pocket where he'd stashed Wendy's resumé, then exited Room 313 before her, ripping the sign off the door on his way out, scrunching it into a ball, and disappearing down the hall, past the long line of applicants.

In spite of the strict instructions to tell no one and bring no one along on the assignment, as soon as Wendy got home, she immediately called Roger and spilled the beans.

"Ginkgo, Chondroitin, and Biloba, Attorneys at Law," Roger answered the phone in his idea of a Latino accent, "José Biloba, esquire, speaking."

"It's me," Wendy whispered.

"What's up, Wenz?" Roger asked.

"I got a job," Wendy said flatly.

"Well, good for you! GOOD. FOR. YOU!" Roger screamed into the receiver.

In an emergency Committee of the Whole meeting, *it was decided that*—for security reasons—Roger should accompany Wendy on her mission, riding shotgun and posing as her deaf, retarded half-brother, and that Wendy's Irish wolfhound, William Butler Yeats, should go along, too, riding in the backseat. Even though Bill was useless as a guard dog and usually got car sick, his presence alone was imposing, his bark alarming.

Out at Hart Field, behind hangar #14, as arranged, a yellow Cessna landed at just after 9:00 p.m. and taxied toward the gate. The pilot deplaned and walked over to Wendy's car.

"Don't say anything," Wendy reminded Roger, speaking through her teeth and rolling down her window. "Not a peep."

"What's your name?" the pilot asked, shining a flashlight in Wendy's face.

"Candy," Wendy replied.

"And who the fuck is that?" he asked, shining the light on Roger. "You were supposed to be alone."

"He's my brother. My . . . um . . . half-brother. My half-wit half-brother. Dwight. I can't leave him alone."

Roger flailed his hands and drooled and rolled his eyes back and banged his head repeatedly against the headrest. "Geega-zeega!" he blubbered. "Geega-zeega! Geega-zeega!"

"Geega-zeega? What the fuck does that mean?" the pilot asked.

"It means . . . Pleased to meet you," Wendy replied. "It's the only word he knows. It means . . . everything."

Suddenly the pilot caught sight of Bill, who had been roused from his sleep and was trying to stand up, rocking the car as he shifted his weight. "And what the fuck is that in the back seat? A horse?"

"That's my dog," Wendy answered.

"What the fuck kind of dog is that?"

"Irish wolfhound," Wendy replied.

"What's his name?"

"Bill."

"Bill? What the fuck kind of name is that for a dog?"

"Well, actually, it's short for William Butler Yeats."

"No shit," the pilot replied, "I LOVE Yeats! *And what rough beast, / its hour come round at last—*"

"Geega-zeega! Geega-zeega!" Roger squealed, and Wendy walloped him with her purse.

"Geega-zeega!" Roger growled, baring his teeth.

A searchlight drew a lazy circle in the sky, a first move, perhaps, in some cosmic game of tic-tac-toe, and in the not-too-far-away distance, a cow mooed, a long baleful moan.

"Geega-zeega!" Roger shouted, slapping the passenger side widow with his palms.

"Tell him to shut the fuck up, will ya?" the pilot said, shining the flashlight again in Roger's face. Roger rolled his eyes and slobbered.

"Bloooba-dah!" Roger shouted at the pilot.

"Hey, you said he only knew one word!" the pilot exclaimed. "He just said a different word."

"Ohmygawd! He did, didn't he?" Wendy responded in her voice of surprise. She was ready to strangle Roger. "He did! He said a new word! Sweetie, you said a new word!" She glared at Roger.

"Flubbermoot!" Roger shouted. "Flubbermoot!"

"I think he's trying to tell us something," said the pilot. "Maybe he's really like an idiot savant, or something."

"No," Wendy said. "He's been tested. He's one-hundred percent idiot. Not an ounce of savant. Believe me. Listen, I thought we weren't supposed to converse."

"Ha! You want to stick to the rules, Candy! You were supposed to be alone, and you show up with an idiot and a horse."

"He's not a horse, he's a dog."

"Okay. An idiot and a dog."

"My strict instructions were to not speak to you at all, and here you are making small talk. This is a business meeting, not a blind date."

"Geega-zeega! Geega-zeega!" Roger chanted rhythmically, while continuing to bang his head.

"Shut up! So . . . where's the envelope?" the pilot asked. Wendy held up the envelope, which she had been sitting on, and the pilot reached for it."

"Not so fast," Wendy said, drawing back the envelope. "Slow down there, cowboy. Where are the flowers?"

"What flowers?" the pilot said and then laughed. "Oh, yeah, the flowers!"

"You idiot," Wendy chastised Roger as the pilot returned to the plane, "I should have left you home. I'm gonna kill you," she said, punching him in the shoulder and hitting him again with her purse while the pilot's back was turned. "You could get us killed. You really are an idiot, ya know that? You really are. If we end up dead, it will be all your fault."

"You were flirting with him!"

"I was not!" Wendy insisted, straightening her wig and applying lip gloss.

"Were, too!"

"Was not!"

"Were, too!"

Wendy got out and opened the trunk, and the transaction was completed.

"See ya," Wendy said quickly, jumping back in the car and locking the door.

"Yeah," the pilot said. And then he leaned down to Wendy's window just as she was rolling it up, and that's when Wendy knew for sure that he was going to kill them.

But he didn't.

He placed his hands on the roof of the car and lowered his head to Wendy's level. "Geega-zeega," he said to Roger, "and you, too, Bill. And, uh, *danke schön*, Candy Cane," he nodded to Wendy, touching the brim of his Pittsburgh Steelers cap. As Wendy continued rolling up the window, he put his hand on it and added, "Did anybody ever tell you

you look like Mary Tyler Moore? I used to love that show—you know, the one where Dick Van Dyke comes in the front door and trips over the ottoman."

Wendy was a sucker for compliments. "That would be *The*—uh—*Dick Van Dyke Show*, I believe," Wendy-the-Smartass responded, her left foot on the break, her right foot ready to smash the gas pedal to the floor.

"Yeah, right. *The Dick Van Dyke Show*. Say," the pilot added, "where are you guys headed? I got a couple of hours to kill, and I'm stuck out here in the middle of nowhere. You wanna go get something to eat or something? A drink maybe? My treat."

He was kind of cute. "Well—"

"Geega-zeega!"

"Listen, tell Clever Hans over there to get a grip. Come on, a bite to eat? Maybe a nice refreshing margarita or a shot of José Cuervo?"

Good gawd! Wendy's favorite poison: tequila. There was definitely some chemistry here. "I don't know. We have a transaction to complete."

"Listen," the pilot assured Wendy. "I can go with you, Candy. I'll protect you. You've got your hands full here."

"Move over, Bill," Wendy said without deliberation. Roger began slapping his fingers against his mouth, making a noise like an Indian whoop.

"He doesn't like strangers," Wendy explained to the pilot. "He can ride in the back with Bill. Bill calms him down. You can sit up front here with me. Besides, Bill might throw up."

Shit. Was it left on Route 26 East or right onto Route 26 West? Wendy had always had a problem with left and right, west and east, north and south. North and south were particularly difficult concepts in a state like West Virginia, where you could be driving straight up the side of a mountain while heading south, or zooming down one, due north. Wendy turned right.

"Where are you going?" the pilot asked.

"I'm not supposed to tell anybody," Wendy replied.

"I can appreciate that," the pilot offered, "but I just thought you might want to know that you're driving in a circle, heading back toward the airport. There's nothing out here for miles, except for a dairy farm, some hillbilly Wild Kingdom, and a defunct Chevron gas station. And I don't think any of them would be in the market for flowers."

"How would you know?" Wendy asked.

"Because I live around here," the pilot said.

"What? You live around here? I thought you were from Colombia?"

"Colombia! Ha! Colombia? Are you kidding?"

"Well, yeah, that's where the flowers are from."

"You think I'd be flying a single-prop plane from Colombia? Hell no, I picked up the *flowers* in Huntington."

"Huntington?"

"Yeah, sometimes it's Huntington, sometimes a private airstrip outside Uniontown, sometimes down in Greenbrier County. It's always different. But I'm from right around Morgantown. Go Mountaineers!"

"How'd you get the job?"

"Ad in the paper."

"Must have own airplane?"

"Precisely. Must have own car?"

"Precisely. Say, how did you know my name is Candy?"

"It's always Candy. If it's a female, it's Candy. If it's a guy, Harpo. But it's almost always a female."

"What happened to the other Candys and Harpos?"

"How the hell would I know?"

Wendy swallowed hard. "What do you think we're delivering?"

"Listen. I don't know, and I don't wanna know. I don't ask questions. I just do my job. I get a phone call. I go pick up the boxes. I deliver the boxes. I pick up some more boxes. I deliver them. I get paid. I go home. It's a good job. No nine-to-five bullshit. No time clock. No asshole in a power tie breathing down my neck. No uniform, no dress code. No performance evaluations. No bottom line. No office politics. No milestones and team meetings. Don't even know who my employer is."

"Hey, what about deliverables?" Candy joked. "But, seriously, what if it's something illegal?"

"What *if*? Are you fucking kidding me? Your brother back there isn't the only idiot in this car. Of course it's something illegal. But all that means is that the government doesn't have its thumb in it. That's all 'illegal' means. It means it's not permitted by THE LAW, not sanctioned by government. It means our Uncle Sam's not getting what he considers to be his fair share. Gotta keep ol' Uncle Sam happy, ya know? It means it's a *tax free* enterprise. What we are, Candy, is entrepreneurs."

"Maybe it's drugs or weapons or some other kind of contraband."

"Duh. This your first time, isn't it, Candy Cane?"

"None of your beeswax."

"Listen. We're in this for the same reason: We both need a job. Society has landed us in this occupation. I bet you have a college degree, don't you? English, right? And where does that leave you? Waiting tables for peanuts or stripping for big bucks—creepy perv slimeballs stuffing $100 bills in your G-string. Listen, I don't blame you one bit."

Wendy didn't know what to say. He was right, after all.

"You know," the pilot went on, "I know this woman who put herself through law school working as a nude housecleaner for some millionaire nudist voyeur. I kid you not."

"Eeeew. That's disgusting," Wendy said, "and perverse."

"Well, you know, it's not really your call, Candy Cane. 'Judge not, lest ye be judged,' as the ol' Good Book says."

"'Neither cast ye your pearls before swine,'" Wendy countered.

"Listen," the pilot continued, "this friend—the nude housecleaner—she said it was a perfectly respectable job—nothing sexual or threatening about it at all. Just a lot of bending over and dusting."

"Puh-leeeeese."

"Think about it: $250, take off your clothes and flick around a feather duster for an hour, or zip on some ugly polyester smock and sling some greasy french fries and cowburgers for minimum wage for eight hours and make $50 for the whole fucking day. Before taxes. And, by the way, you know cattle ranching is responsible for the disappearance of the Brazilian rainforest."

Wendy was silent, thinking.

"And if it's drugs, the way I look at it is like then we're doing a service. We're part of a service organization, I figure. Sort of like the Red Cross or United Way. We don't even know what we've got in the trunk. Yeah, I'm guessing drugs. Drugs to get some poor pillbillies high.

But you know what? The rich have their own drugs. They've got their prescription drugs. Their legal highs. They got their legal dealers. Hey, John F. Kennedy wasn't getting any daily vitamin-B12 shots from Dr. Feelgood. He was getting speed—fifty milligrams of amphetamines per injection. You know Truman Capote was getting those shots, too, and you know what he said about them?"

"What?"

"He said, 'You feel like Superman. Ideas come at the speed of light. You can go seventy-two hours without even a coffee break.' Vitamin-B, my ass."

"But, what if we kill somebody—I mean, indirectly, inadvertently. Still . . . I mean, what if we're involved in some drug cartel or we're delivering weapons for some Mountain Militia that's planning to blow up the Pentagon? What if we're decoys for some sting operation? Do you have any idea what the prison sentence is for drug trafficking?"

"Oh, and like blowing up the Pentagon with its Masters of War would be a bad idea? And, Candy, there are occupational hazards in every job. Take, for instance, coal mining or convenience store clerk. You work at a 7-11, man, your life is on the line from the minute you clock in to the minute you're out of there. Most dangerous job on the planet. I kid you not.

"And what if we, like, worked for Philip Morris or Ronald Ray-Gun?" the pilot went on. "That would be more—uhm—*honorable*, more *upstanding*, you think? Or what about Union Carbide? At least 3,000 dead in Bhopal last year, and nobody knows the long-term effect on those exposed to the gas leak. And Union Carbide showing a profit at the end of this year! You know, Candy, you could probably get a job in their corporate offices in Charleston. P.R., maybe?"

Silence. A few minutes passed and then the pilot spoke again. "Say, what do you think back there, Geega-Zeega? You've been pretty quiet. Horse got your tongue?"

"Geega-zeega!"

"Hey, the Voice of Reason has regained consciousness! How ya doin' back there, buddy? Listen, Candy," the pilot continued, "I really think you better make a U-turn. You're probably supposed to go to Angie's Good Time, right?

Wendy didn't answer.

"Listen. It's in the opposite direction. Trust me on this."

Wendy pulled into a rutted dirt road with a hand-painted plywood sign that said HOVATTER'S WILD KINGDOM. A lion roared. Something screamed. A peacock? A wildcat? A chimp? Bill barked. The Horizon shook. Wendy backed up and peeled out in the opposite direction.

Angie's Good Time had just come into view when Bill began to gag.

"Oh, shit," the pilot said, "he's not going to barf, is he?"

"Roll the window down! Quick! Roll the window down!" Wendy hollered as she swerved into the gravel parking lot. "He just needs some fresh air. Listen, you guys get out and walk Bill around the side while I drive around back. I'm supposed to be alone."

"Geega-zeega! Geega-zeega!"

"Out!" Wendy said to Roger. "I'll be right back. Take Bill's leash. If I'm not back out front in five minutes, come get me."

"We'll be right here," the pilot said, climbing out. "I think I smell food. I definitely smell french fries."

Behind the building, Wendy pulled up to the cement stoop and honked the horn. A man in army fatigues and combat boots came out and walked over to Wendy's car. "You Candy?" he asked.

"That would be me," Wendy said. "You Groucho?"

"You bet your life," the guy answered. "Where's the shit?"

"In the trunk," Wendy replied.

"Open it."

"Give me the money first," Wendy said coolly.

He handed her a roll of bills, and Wendy counted them. She squint-ed at the picture of the president on the bill. He looked a little bit like William Hurt, a very old William Hurt.

"McKinley," Groucho said as he observed Wendy scrutinizing the bill. "He was assassinated, you know."

Wendy gulped and opened the trunk. She kept the car running while Groucho removed the boxes. Around the corner of Angie's Good Time, Roger and the pilot leaned against the grill of a monster truck, smoking a joint, while Bill peed on one of the monster tires.

"Geega-zeega," they both giggled, piling back into the car with Bill.

In front of the First National Bank, Wendy parallel parked, no easy maneuver with Bill the only thing visible in the rearview mirror. She deposited the moneybag in the night depository box and jumped back in the car.

"Whatcha get paid?" the pilot asked.

"$500," Wendy answered.

"*Moi aussi*. Come on, let's go out. I don't have to be back at Hart Field until midnight. I could use a drink and a bite to eat. Let's go to that transvestite karaoke bar, Vice Versa, across the street. Ever been there? I've always wanted to check it out. What say, Geega-Zeega?"

Roger smiled.

"What about Bill?"

"Come on, he'll be fine. Look, Trigger's asleep."

"Well . . . I guess . . . he does like to sleep in the car." Roger was already out of the car and skipping across the street.

Inside Vice Versa, the pilot ordered the nachos supreme platter and a pitcher of frozen margaritas with three glasses. On stage, Tammy Wynette in copious lace and fringe was belting out "Stand By Your Man." Roger excused himself and Wendy took off her wig.

"Nice hair," the pilot remarked to Wendy. "That a wig, too?"

"So funny I forgot to laugh," Wendy said, laughing.

"So, uhm, what's your real name?" he asked.

"What's yours?"

"Peter Pan."

Wendy laughed again. "Yeah, right. And I'm Wendy."

The pilot poured them each a margarita. "Ugga-wugga, meatball," he said, clinking his glass to Wendy's.

"Ugga-wugga," Wendy clinked back.

"Here's to jobs." He took a big drink.

"Yeah, jobs."

Wendy's mind drifted back to her freshman Econ 101 class and *The Wealth of Nations*, which had led to a discussion of abundance and scarcity, competition and the optimal unemployment rate. It was the only occasion ever when Wendy had raised her hand.

"You mean a certain percentage of unemployment is *desirable?*" Wendy asked. "How can unemployment be *desirable?*"

"May I remind you, Miss Long," the professor answered, "that we're talking about a free-market economy? A modest amount of unemployment increases the competition for jobs."

"The greatest good," another student called out.

"But if everyone had a job—" Wendy continued.

"Miss Long, dear Miss Long," the professor interrupted, "we're talking about capitalism here, not socialism. We're discussing reality here, not some Never-Never Land." And Wendy shut up.

Tammy Wynette was taking her bow, and who should appear on stage but Roger, swaying his hips and snapping his fingers, holding the mic in his signature sissy-grip and singing.

> *Sha na na na, sha na na na na,*
> *Sha na na na, sha na na na na,*

"Geega-zeega!" the pilot shouted, then sounded an ear-splitting, two-fingered wolf whistle. Leaning close to Wendy, he cupped his hands and spoke into her ear, "Hey, your brother said another new word!"

> *when I get back to the house*
> *I hear the woman's mouth*
> *Preaching and a crying,*
> *Tell me that I'm lying,*

On the chorus, everyone in the smoky bar joined in—patrons, barkeep, waitrons, all—yipping and yelping and yowling like every manner of coyote, dog, and wolf:

> *Yip yip yip yip yip yip yip yip*
> *Mum mum mum mum mum mum*
> *Get a job!*

It was another Friday night downtown in a small city in Appalachia. Family Dollar on one corner, homeless shelter next door. A bail bondsman next to that, with t-shirts in the window advertising, I'M FREE! FREE AT LAST! County jail a block away. State job service, home confinement correction program, and parole offices in the old A&P. Church of God in the defunct Warner Theater. County court house, Hot Spot, pawn shop. Salvation Army, Volunteers of America, Goodwill, Christian Help, Dunkin' Donuts. *Guns & Ammo! Guns & Ammo!* Biscuit World, Tanning World, Baby World. Adult Toy Shop. *Must be 18 and show I.D. to enter.* Club Z. The Piercing Palace. Holy Hookah. *Cash on the Spot for Your Car Title.* Fanci-Funki Nails. Discount Jewelry, Discount Liquor. Karaoke Every Night. *What Would Jesus Do?* Lotto King! Pizza King! Porn King! *Girls! Girls! Girls!* Abandoned federal post office building surrounded by weeds, dog turds, and trash. More bars, lawyers, tattoo parlors, guns and ammo, boarded up storefronts spray painted with graffiti.

Inside Vice Versa, Wendy drained her second margarita and the pilot nodded to the waiter, pointing to the empty pitcher.

"This is great," the pilot said, putting his arm around Wendy's chair and leaning toward her. "I mean it." He licked his thumb and dabbed at Wendy's salt moustache.

"You know, that idiot brother of yours is a real trip," the pilot continued. "He almost had me fooled for a minute back there, back at the airport." The pilot sucked the coarse salt off his thumb and licked his lips. "You know, maybe we can all do this again some time. What say, Candy Cane—or Wendy—or whatever you name is?"

"Geega-zeega," Wendy hiccupped.

"Flubbermoot," the pilot whispered in her ear. "*Blooooooba-daaaaah.*"

✦ The Man in the Woods ✦

Every evening after a small dinner exactly like the small dinners his wife had prepared every evening for over fifty years—a lean cut of sale meat: boneless, skinless chicken breast or pork chop with the fat trimmed away, a limp fillet of flounder or tilapia; a starch in the form of one medium-sized baked, boiled, or microwaved potato, one cup of cooked Minute Rice, or two boiled potato-cheese pierogies; a green vegetable, preferably broccoli or Brussels sprouts; a side dish of applesauce or fruit cocktail (the canned variety with plump gooseberries treading heavy syrup)—plus two or three glasses of red wine substituted for the traditional tall glass of unsweetened iced tea—Thomas Davies took himself and his little dog Evangeline for a walk.

The dog was a toy Manchester terrier with particularly expressive ears, who had belonged to Thomas's late wife, Virginia. Virginia had doted on the little dog and had not disciplined it properly when it was a puppy, as all terriers must be disciplined else they develop what is known as "small-dog syndrome" wherein the small dog believes itself to be a large canine breed such as a Rottweiler and that it is pack leader to humans and, henceforth, displays unduly aggressive and dominant behavior.

Evangeline was so inclined.

After dinner and after Evangeline had licked Thomas's plate and after Thomas had placed the dishes in the dishwasher and tidied the kitchen (Evangeline growling and tugging at his trousers' cuff the whole time), off they went, Thomas and Evangeline, crossing Dorsey Avenue, then winding through the broken paths of East Oak Grove Cemetery and out the cemetery's south gate and down Callen Avenue toward White Park, the reservoir, and the river.

This evening's walk was particularly pleasant because even though it was late July, the heat was not unbearable, and there had been abundant rainfall throughout the summer months so that the grass was not scorched and breeding hay mites as it often did during the Dog Days. And everything was blooming profusely—the slender orange daylilies along the cemetery's rim; the random overgrown Rose-of-Sharons, planted here and there many years ago by grieving survivors; the sweet mimosas waving their feathery, malodorous arms; the sturdy geraniums congregated in substantial stone urns, suggesting permanence.

A mockingbird seemed to be leading Thomas and Evangeline on their way, flitting from obelisk to obelisk in front of them, gesturing coyly with its fanned tail, like a geisha. A large, dirigible-shaped cloud portended rain, but that was just some meteorological practical joke. Where the cloud had come from and what it was composed of if not rain that gave it its ominous but beautiful blue-gray hue and how it came to be floating above the cemetery like the Goodyear blimp was anybody's guess. Rain was not even alluded to in the extended forecast.

Thomas paused at Virginia's grave. He leaned forward and stuck his index finger into the small clay pot of white begonias. The soil was still damp; no need to water. All last evening it had rained, a silent, persistent rain, and the plot was in the shade of one of the cemetery's oldest willows, having been planted by Virginia's forebears before the Civil War. Thomas stared at the deep-cut letters and dates chiseled into the polished pink granite of Virginia's gravestone as Evangeline sniffed about at the end of her lead.

In three days, it would be a year since Virginia's death. His own name was engraved next to Virginia's on the stone, with his birth date, followed by an elegant en dash and adequate blank space for a month, a two-digit day, a four-digit year. Around the stone, Virginia's ancestors' names called out—Nell, Miriam, Waitman, Stella, Cora, Francis, Earl,

Moira, Nancy Jane, Mary Ann, Ned, Charles, Rees, May, Evan, Samuel, Morgan, Edris—all flatly declaring their varying stitches of time on weathered, leaning markers, some with faces as dissolved as damp sugar cubes. Many were children, many young women having died in childbirth, "infant son" or "infant daughter" buried beside them. Some had perished during the Spanish influenza and the great World Wars. One was a missionary who had been murdered in China; Thomas knew the story, passed down four generations. Two others—newlyweds setting out to homestead in Oregon—had drowned in the sinking of the steamboat *Brother Jonathan* off the California coast on July 30, 1865. A tribute to the young couple, etched into the plinth of an angel cantilevered forward like a ship's masthead, read:

> *Yet mourn we not as they*
> *whose spirit's light is quenched.*
> *All is not here of our beloved and bless'd*
> *We leave the sleepers with their God to rest.*

"A mother's lament," the inscription said. All these lives, Thomas mused, all these tragedies and interruptions and finalities. And now Virginia there among them with her small pot of white begonias and polished pink stone behind the curtain of the old weeping willow.

Spirit's light. Sometimes, especially on a starry night, Thomas looked up and could imagine Virginia floating about like a paper kite, flying like Wendy in *Peter Pan*. Secretly, he did not believe that Virginia was really dead. He was giving her a year to come back or send him some sign. Oh yes, it would be a miracle. She would walk in the door while he was watching the news on television or she'd be standing there at the kitchen sink peeling potatoes when he walked in, and she'd tell him about her great adventure and what a mistake it had been—all of it. It would be a fantastic story, a miracle, but really, weren't fairy tales and myths and religions rich with miracles? The raising of the dead, the walking on water, the multiplication of the loaves and fishes, the turning of water into wine, beasts and frogs transformed into princes, gods turning themselves into swans and crows into witches, talking serpents. Helen of Troy and Jesus of Nazareth — half human, half divine. Persephone ascending from the underworld every spring. Orpheus trudging down into Hades and taking Eurydice by her little hand. Cows jumping over the moon.

Oh, yes, he'd been the one who had found Virginia in the garage and called 911, and he'd read the coroner's report and he'd stood by Virginia's closed casket for the long afternoon and evening at Derings Funeral Home and the next day at the service and burial, and during the lowering down of the casket into the amazingly box-like hole lined with bright green cloth meant to look like grass. He'd said the Lord's Prayer and heard the benediction and let himself be led by his daughter and her husband back to the limousine. The green cloth, he was certain, was designed to obscure the damp clods, the diligent worms.

"I can walk," Thomas had said to his daughter, heading off by himself in the direction of the house.

But Jill had caught up with him. "Oh, no, Daddy," his daughter insisted, "it wouldn't look right."

Nearly fifty, Jill's hair was gray now, too, like his, like Virginia's, and it all seemed so peculiar. He saw himself as a boy in short pants, walking behind his grandfather's casket, holding his mother's gloved hand, the twenty-one gun salute, his grandmother in widow's weeds, fainting, everyone dressed in black.

Virginia's graveside service, however, was colorful. Jill wore a bright blue dress and a broad-brimmed floppy hat Thomas thought showy and inappropriate. Someone was dressed in a gaudy fluttering skirt, someone else in ugly, vibrant pink. Propriety had vanished long ago.

At first, Thomas thought he would not live out the year. Now he imagined himself drawing his last breath on exactly the same day as Virginia, on the anniversary of her death.

"But, it's only a stone's throw," he'd said to Jill when she insisted he ride in the limousine.

"Please, Daddy, don't make a scene."

And so Thomas climbed back into the plush, orange zest-scented limousine with its box of generic Kleenex strategically placed between the seats, watching the silent markers pass, the John Deere front-end loader lurching out from behind the maintenance shed without even the decency to wait for the procession to pass, charging like a rhinoceros toward Virginia's open grave.

Evangeline, impatient as always at any and all dawdling, shook her head, purposefully jingling her tags, and gave a tug on her lead. Thomas retrieved a small, smooth stone from his pocket—one selected from his collection of skipping stones, which he kept in a large brass pot on the hearth. He laid the stone along the base of Virginia's tombstone, along with the hundreds of others, and continued on his way, Evangeline pulling at the end of her lead, tail up, ears twitching.

Soon he was at the cemetery's south entrance and relieved to have made his way through the graveyard without encountering his former colleague, Jacob Hirsch, the philosophy professor emeritus who often took his evening constitution with his basset hound, Descartes, approaching the cemetery from the opposite direction as Thomas and Evangeline. Jacob, though sincere and congenial, always tried to engage Thomas in a philosophical debate. Long widowed, Jacob was even friendlier after Virginia's passing, as if Thomas had been inducted into the same secret fraternal order or was afflicted with the same debilitating disease.

Thomas avoided him at all costs.

If their paths did cross, Jacob usually altered his route and accompanied Thomas and Evangeline on the remainder of their walk, Evangeline prancing ahead, Descartes lumbering after them, Jacob talking ceaselessly all the way to Thomas's gate and lingering there some evenings until the sun had set and the lightning bugs were waist high. But Thomas refused to open the gate and invite Jacob and Descartes in. Even the most mundane topic—the weather, the price of some commodity—Jacob could transform into a most lengthy, abstract discussion revolving around the origin, the nature, the methods, and limits of human understanding.

"Why do we accept that chicken thighs are worth 99¢ per pound?" Jacob might ask. "Is it because we have a coupon, because we read the sign over the refrigerated case, because when the cashier scans the bar code, 99¢ per pound is the price registered? Or is it because we trust in our monetary system, in our system of weights and measures, in our understanding of the intrinsic value of chicken thighs and because we are motivated to purchase them at the price we deem reasonable in relationship to the money in our pocket and the gnawing sensation in our stomachs?" On and on and on.

He was nuts, Thomas long ago concluded. Philosophy—and possibly English—were the only departments where Jacob Hirsch could have found a home and actually been rewarded and encouraged in his nonsense, earning the rank of full professor. It was a fine line—that was certain—between wisdom and blather. And although Thomas was dismissive of Jacob's queries, he usually found himself playing along, but after each conversation his head was spinning, his mind racing, and even after his customary nightcap of a cup of beef bouillon laced with a hearty shot of Jameson's, Thomas couldn't sleep.

He sighed with relief when he reached the end of the cemetery path and started down Callen Avenue with Jacob and Descartes nowhere in sight.

Callen Avenue, however, was another test. The first block was the stretch where the Miller sisters—Martha and Rose—lived, Rose widowed and Martha an old maid. The Miller sisters had grown up with Virginia and, like Virginia, had lived in the neighborhood their entire lives. On Callen Avenue, a war was being waged between the sisters, the ammunition flowers. Almost overnight, it seemed, a deep, curved flowerbed laden with a reddish mulch that resembled bacon bits had replaced the narrow strip of marigolds and liatris that summer after summer had lined the path from the sidewalk to Rose Popovich's front porch.

Early one morning in the middle of June, a lime green truck with a caricature of an ape in a pair of overalls pushing a lawnmower and the name YARD APE in yellow letters underneath it parked in front of Rose's house, and two shirtless, deeply tanned young men in lime green caps emblazoned with the same logo unloaded a variety of digging tools, rakes, and wheelbarrows, and an enormous cooler with a spigot, and set to work transforming Rose's front yard into something out of *House & Garden*.

By the end of the day, the wide, flag-shaped flowerbed was complete, edged with sparkly white stones. White impatiens and red and purple petunias occupied the bed, simulating a garish Stars and Stripes, and

Rose proudly appeared on the front porch in a Hawaiian muumuu to hang a new welcome flag. The new flag was bright yellow, silkscreened with the image of a soldier with an M-16 rifle in one hand, a little girl holding his other hand. SUPPORT OUR TROOPS, the flag demanded.

Across the street, Martha Miller—Rose's sister—drew the blinds and rolled her eyes. *Praise God and pass the ammunition,* she said to herself, turning her back on the scene and heading down the hall, toward the whistling tea kettle and the telephone.

The next afternoon, Martha, with the help of a neighbor boy, was unloading from her station wagon three large cement flower boxes, one fifty-pound bag of sand, six bags of Miracle-Gro potting soil, four flats of annuals, and a fire plug-size statue of St. Francis, complete with birds. Martha worked well into the night, planting ivy geraniums, trailing dusty miller, bocopa, and wave petunias. St. Francis took his place by the porch stairs, cement arm raised, as if releasing or catching a bird nesting in the eaves or hailing the soldier and his charge across the street.

Thomas dreaded an encounter with Martha or Rose, both of whom demonstrated what he considered to be an unhealthy, competitive interest in him since his wife's death. Virginia and both sisters were master gardeners, and for years, Virginia and Martha had been in the same bookclub. After their monthly bookclub meetings, Virginia always returned home with tales about Martha and her unusual book picks: *The Celestine Prophecy, The Afterdeath Journals of William James, The Search for Bridey Murphy,* books which baffled Virginia but in which Thomas took a lively interest, often reading long passages of them while Virginia was out.

He would almost like to know Martha, to sit down and talk to her about her esoteric book selections.

After Virginia's untimely death, both sisters began to stop by, one at a time, often with a baked good or casserole. Rose was the better cook, but Thomas found her overbearing. He took more to Martha, the pudgy, bookish peacenik with the dimples and easy smile, but in her presence, Thomas felt awkward and sometimes hid in the hallway if he spotted her opening the gate and coming down the walk. After she'd rung the doorbell twice, and Thomas was certain she'd left, he hurried to the spare bedroom upstairs where he could stand against the wall and watch her walk toward home. Through the cemetery she walked with her pleasant gait, and Thomas watched her until the path curved. Then he moved in front of the window and watched until she disappeared. The tinfoil-covered foodstuff was always left on the cobbler's bench by the front door.

Both sisters had offered to care for Virginia's perennials and had given Thomas detailed advice about mulching and pruning, splitting and transplanting, but Thomas did not care for gardening, and he let the flowerbeds go. Still, lilies and irises had bloomed among the weeds, as they would for years to come.

Thomas had never liked the outdoors and had always been especially frightened in the woods. He was afraid of the dark and of open spaces as well as confined ones like elevators and enclosed public stairways. At the age of ten, he had been sent, unwillingly, to Boy Scout camp where he was terrified of the night sounds—the mournful hoot of owls and the eerie call of whippoorwills, the skittering of squirrels and the scraping of branches on the cabin roof. He hated insects, reptiles, and amphibians, and he loathed the murky pond the boys were meant to swim in, its muddy, oozing bottom and slimy stones. He would not go near the end of the dock, where the other boys did their belly-flops and cannonballs. He feared bears and beyond the campfire's glow, how easily a tree or stump took on an ursine form. Will-o'-the-wisp came alive in the marsh, a seething thousand-eyed monster. He was afraid of snakes—all varieties, including the garter—and was certain they lived in the latrines and would strike at the most inopportune moments or that they would fall out of trees and land entangled around his neck, as he'd seen in *Tarzan* movies.

At camp he was quickly identified as a sissy, singled out, and terrorized by the camp bullies: a salamander and once a garter snake tucked into his sleeping bag, a nightcrawler in the bottom of his bowl of Grapenuts, a dead tadpole stuffed into the toe of his shoe. Every night, Thomas cried silently in his bed, never sleeping, and after six days was sent home with a fever, after collapsing from physical exhaustion.

Virginia, however, had always been fearless. She loved nature and the outdoors. She—along with Rose and Martha—had been Campfire Girls, and when Jill was little, Virginia was a Brownie and then a Girl Scout leader, taking the girls on treks and overnighters and birding expeditions.

Virginia was always ready for a hike in the woods, a camping trip, an outdoor picnic, a walk to the reservoir with one of her various dogs. When she was younger, in the winter she cross-country skied, and in the summer she enjoyed kayaking and whitewater rafting, and on her fiftieth birthday she signed up for scuba diving lessons. But Thomas stayed home. Something about the outdoors always stirred in him a mild panic, and those outdoor activities Virginia loved so much were the kinds of things, he used to joke, that they made you do all day, every day, in Hell.

In recent years, though, after his heart attack the day just before his seventy-third birthday and the doctor's orders that he walk for at least an hour daily, Thomas began to accompany Virginia and Evangeline on their daily walk, the route Thomas and Evangeline were following now: a three-mile loop, through the cemetery, down Callen Avenue, up Mississippi, through the White Park reservoir trail to the waterfall and back. They'd walked this route nearly every day — rain or shine — for three years, and slowly, Thomas began to look forward to the time outside, especially in the winter when the trees were bare and there was a more open feeling in the woods, and they were bundled in their scarves and galoshes, Evangeline in the thick red sweater Jill had knitted for her. It was because of Virginia, so at home and confident outside, pointing out plants and birds and trees and animal tracks, leaves and stones and shadows, that Thomas enjoyed the walk, but still, even alongside Virginia, he was always relieved to see the cemetery come back into view and the familiar red roof of their house just beyond. To open the gate, the door, to step safely inside.

Today was Thomas's lucky day; he made it down the long block of Callen Avenue without running into either of the Miller sisters. Gigantic sun-flowers formed a row along Martha's iron fence. Next to a large hibiscus, a new welcome flag with a peace sign hung from a wrought iron stanchion, the inside of each slice of the peace pie a colorful wildflower.

Thomas always felt a tinge of trepidation as he approached the White Park entrance sign and the trail that led around the reservoir to the waterfall and, eventually, down to the river. The trepidation was a mild version of the same terror he'd felt at that summer camp when he was a boy. The White Park reservoir trail was a lovely, well-maintained, and level path with a foot bridge over a shallow ravine, frequented by joggers and dog walkers and bicyclists, but often Thomas and Evangeline walked the entire mile loop around the big sycamore and the waterfall overlook without seeing anyone. Along this trail, here and only here, did Thomas hope for someone familiar to pass—even Jacob Hirsch—someone he could nod to or someone who would comment on how cute Evangeline was or offer some pleasantry about the weather.

This evening as Thomas approached the trail, he noted the absence of cars in the small parking lot and the long trail receding to its vanishing point without a person in sight. The familiar feeling of quiet dread swept over him, but Evangeline made the turn automatically and tugged on her lead, and Thomas entered the trail, walking quickly. It would only take fifteen minutes to reach the old sycamore and then turn back.

The sun hung low over the reservoir, illuminating the water where a few picturesque mallards floated about placidly as decoys.

Near the turnabout, Thomas saw a figure move in the woods. A man behind a tree. Thomas's immediate thought was to turn and start back, but he steeled himself and walked on. Only a few more feet and he would be at the turnabout. Something within him, some devil-may-care attitude since Virginia's passing, propelled him.

As he rounded the turnabout marked by the big sycamore, the man stepped out in front of him. He was a big man, in his fifties perhaps, in baggy khaki trousers and a dark blue t-shirt. His hair was shaved close to his head.

Thomas's heartbeat quickened.

"Hello," the man said, "my name is Paul. May I walk with you?"

What could Thomas say? "Certainly," a voice that was Thomas's but not Thomas's answered.

"I'm just a lonely man, a homeless man," Paul said, "a transient man. I have no home. No family. No job. No place to live."

Thomas's heart began to pound, his legs to quiver.

"Times are hard," Thomas said, quickening his pace.

To his surprise, Evangeline did not respond at all to the man but kept trotting ahead as if he did not exist. The path ahead seemed long, and no one was in sight. Thomas did not turn to look at the man, who now walked beside him, a little too closely. Out of the corner of his eye, Thomas observed the man's brown oxfords and his trousers, which appeared worn and tattered.

"I have no place to live," the man repeated. "I like the woods. It's peaceful. I stay here during the day. May I ask your name?"

"Thomas." Thomas said flatly. "My name is Thomas." He did not offer his surname.

"Do you sleep at Bartlett House?" Thomas asked, trying to keep the conversation moving along as he anxiously looked ahead for the path's entrance, for the patch of light and sidewalk, willing the path to open up again onto Mississippi Avenue. Bartlett House was the homeless shelter downtown, a good thirty-minute walk in the opposite direction from Thomas's home.

"Yes," Paul said, "I sleep there, but I come here. They make you leave by 8:00 a.m., and I come here."

"But there are other places downtown," Thomas said. "The Friendship Room," he added. He knew of the Friendship Room because Virginia had been on the board of directors. It was adjacent to the public library, a facility where homeless people could spend the day in organized activities—watching movies, doing crafts, reading books and magazines, talking to trained counselors. Coffee and healthy snacks were always available.

"I don't like it there," Paul said. "Forgive me, sir, I'm not bothering you, am I? You don't mind if I walk with you, Thomas? May I call you Thomas?"

"Oh, no," Thomas said, walking faster.

"I don't like the Friendship Room," Paul continued. "There's trouble there. I don't like people. I don't like to be around people. I don't like it downtown. I feel agitated around people. I'm afraid I might hurt someone."

Fear raced down Thomas's spine like a zipper. He could almost feel Paul's hand on the back of his neck, see the glint of pointed steel. He was almost trotting now. His heart was pounding and he was short of breath.

"I don't like young people," Paul said. "I like older people like yourself. There's another place," Paul continued, "a Christian place. But it's only open sporadically."

For some reason, Thomas was surprised that Paul used the word "sporadically." He knew the place Paul was referring to, Haven of Hope. It was another daytime shelter supported by his own church, First Methodist. Virginia and the Miller sisters worked in the kitchen of Haven of Hope on holidays, preparing turkey and baked ham dinners.

Thomas didn't go to church anymore, now that Virginia was gone, but he still tithed, mailing his check like clockwork the first of every month. He was never a believer, just a believer in tradition and goodwill. He had been raised a Methodist. Like Virginia. Service, he believed, was the root of religion. And the Golden Rule: *Do unto others . . .* But Thomas didn't *do* like Virginia; he contributed to the cause but never really embraced it. It was not in his character to participate.

What an unlikely couple they were, Thomas had always thought, he and Virginia. Virginia so engaged—in nature and the world—himself so withdrawn. Out of fear, out of something. But she was the only woman he'd ever loved.

"Do you have a job?" Thomas asked, filling the momentary silence. Paul walked easily beside him, Evangeline ahead.

"No," Paul said, "I don't have a job. I'm on disability. I have a troubled mind. I can't work. I have so many regrets. So many—"

His voice trailed off.

Thomas wondered how the man survived, where he had been, how he lived. He registered Paul's close-cropped hair, the scars on his scalp. He recalled how someone had told him that when prisoners were released from the nearby penitentiary just over the West Virginia-Pennsylvania border, they were given a bus ticket to Morgantown. In Morgantown, there was the homeless shelter, the free clinic for the homeless, the Salvation Army, Volunteers of America, Goodwill, the soup kitchens offering three square meals a day, Friendship Room and Haven of Hope, and Christian Help, the facility that gave free clothes to the homeless . . ., all within blocks of each other downtown. And there were the old hobo camps, too, he'd heard of, along the river.

"My father was a big man," Paul said, "an angry man. A mean man. I lived in Germany for seven years when I was a boy."

Thomas imagined for a second the father, a figure like Robert De Niro in *This Boy's Life*, and he wondered if Paul was a veteran.

"Have you served in the armed forces?" Thomas asked.

"Oh, no," Paul answered. "I'm mentally disabled. I suffer from mental illness. I'm just a lonely man, a sick and homeless, wandering man. An indigent man. I have no home, no family, no job."

Although Thomas was terrified by the man's presence, he noted that there was nothing threatening about Paul. He had a kind voice, a calm demeanor, and Evangeline, who was usually cautious and on-guard with strangers, continued to pay him no mind.

They should be to the end of the trail now, Thomas kept thinking. The road should be in view, but the trail seemed to stretch into infinity, and Thomas had the sickening sense that it would go on forever, that he'd entered some surreal realm where every step was like a step on a treadmill, the trail scrolling under his feet, his progress negligible.

Finally, they reached the White Park entrance sign and the pavement. The sidewalk and street were bare.

"Well, good-bye, then," Thomas said quickly. He turned toward Paul, and Paul extended his right hand. Thomas hesitated but took it. Paul's hand was amazingly warm and soft. Like a woman's. Paul placed his left hand on top of Thomas's hand and held it firmly. And although Thomas felt a pleasing warmth radiating from Paul's hands, he wanted to jerk his hand back, but didn't. He looked into Paul's face and noted his sad brown eyes, a long scar on his temple, the full lips and missing teeth.

"Good-bye, brother," Paul said, "and God bless you."

No one had ever called Thomas brother.

"Good-bye to you," Thomas said. "And God bless you," he added.

Thomas had never said that either, unless someone had sneezed.

Thomas hurried along, afraid to look back. He wanted to turn to see if Paul was watching or following him or if he had retreated back into the woods. He began to wonder if Paul sometimes slept in the woods, perhaps on one of the benches at the waterfall lookout. The thought of a night spent alone in the woods terrified Thomas, and he shuddered.

He rehearsed in his head the things Paul had said, the repetition, the fearful thing.

Thomas took a circuitous route home, afraid of being followed. Although the neighborhood was familiar — he'd lived in Virginia's family home for almost half a century now — Thomas felt as if he'd entered some strange, new world. On Callen Avenue, he passed whirligigs of frantic ducks going nowhere; cement geese in hideous gingham capes and caps; an enormous ceramic frog dancing a jig and playing a fiddle; a life-size wooden cutout of a fat woman bending over, displaying ruffled, polka-dotted pantaloons on her ample behind.

Thomas felt disoriented and anxious, as if he was marooned on a movie set and the conversation he'd just had with Paul was the dialogue from some morality play he'd been dropped into. Evangeline at the end of her lead was like a tether, and Thomas felt grateful for her, feeling he might float away without his hand on the leash that held this ten-pound, feisty anchor.

When Martha Miller's side yard came into view, Thomas felt a wave of relief, but as he walked along the wrought-iron fence line, he felt even more agitated by the carmine-colored hibiscus, their blossoms like bloody dinner plates, and the sunflowers with their heads the size of toilet seats. Only when he had crossed the cemetery and reached his own gate did he turn. No one was in sight.

Safe inside, Thomas poured himself a stiff shot of Jameson's, forgoing the bouillon, and sat down at the dining room table, a place he'd never sat since Virginia's passing. He gave Evangeline a Frosty Paw, and the only sound was her licking and the scoot of the Dixie cup across the kitchen floor until the dessert cup was wedged in a corner where she could get down to business.

The house grew dark, but Thomas didn't turn on any lights. He went to the kitchen and picked up the bottle of whiskey and brought it to the dining room table and poured himself another shot. Gradually, the fear left him, and he began to cry. After a while, Thomas began to wonder if Paul was real or if he was an apparition, if he'd imagined the whole encounter. For a moment, he even considered that Paul was an angel.

Thomas thought he might gather up some of his things — the Burberry coat he'd hardly worn, the Irish fisherman's sweater Jill had spent years knitting him and which he'd never worn, the insulated socks she'd given him for Christmas — and make a care package for Paul, five folded twenties tucked in the coat's inside pocket, and drop them off at Bartlett House, but what would that do? Ease his conscience? He could have been more cordial. He could have offered to walk Paul to the homeless shelter. Or given him a ride. He could have given him money right then and there; he never left the house without his wallet.

The fact was, Thomas knew, he had finally encountered in the woods what he had dreaded all his life. That night, he finished the bottle of Jameson's and stumbled upstairs and fell into bed and sobbed into his pillow, *Come back, Come back*, and in his dreams the man in the woods returned again and again. Sometimes the man in the woods was Paul, only dressed in Thomas's Lacoste shirt and Ecco shoes, and sometimes the man in the woods was Thomas himself, clothed in tattered khakis, his hair shorn, dentures missing. And in one vivid fragment of a dream, Thomas turned toward the man in the woods and the man was no longer a man, he was Virginia, but when Thomas took his beloved in his arms, she was not Virginia at all. She was Paul.

✦ Personal Effects ✦

Okay. Alrighty, then. Let's start with the shoes.

No. No. No. No. No. No. No. Oh, gawd, no! None of these will do. No. No, no Dansko clogs. No. You cannot keep the lizard cowboy boots. Yes, I know. I can see they're like new. Yes, I can imagine what they must have cost. But they just won't work. Trust me on this: there will be no "Achy Breaky Heart," no line dancing, where you're going. And no, I'm afraid not. Not even the red Chucks. No! No espadrilles! Definitely, no espadrilles. Espadrilles are out of the question. The black pumps, are you kidding? So you got them in Italy on your honeymoon. Let me ask you this: when was the last time you wore them? See? I know. But that's not important. That, too, will fall away. We're concerned here with only four things: comfort, functionality, safety, and weight. CFSW. Remember that. Everything must be CFSW. Well, the saddle shoes. Almost . . . but . . . no. Take them off. You will need a good pair of sturdy, all-season boots. Good support. Waterproof. You will wear them everywhere, everyday. Yes, perhaps a pair of Harley Davidson or Doc Marten engineer boots would do. Something comfortable, sturdy, protective, something you can walk in and sleep in. No, no slippers. You will not need slippers where you're going.

LINGERIE

Lingerie? Are you kidding? No. No bras or cammies or underpants. No Spanxx! No one will notice. Trust me on this. No. One. Will. Care. Here, you can take two of these, these sleeveless leotards. Black. All season. Put one on. I am *not* looking. You'll need two t-shirts, too. Cotton or poly-cotton, long-sleeved, one insulated, a turtleneck. I DON'T CARE WHAT COLOR!

CLOTHES

Dresses, skirts, blouses—all this silk and velvet? Linen? Oh, please! Linen? Bamboo? I thought that was for placemats. Organic cotton? Listen. It's all useless. No, you cannot take the Eileen Fisher velvet waistcoat, the cutaway swallowtail tuxedo jacket, or the 1940s corduroy smoking jacket with the paisley satin lining. No, not the cropped boiled wool jacket with the hammered silver buttons. I don't care if it was your mother's! This flimsy Banana Republic wiggle dress? Are you fuckin' kidding me? ABSOLUTELY NOT! You wouldn't last a day in that. Kimonos? No way! I suppose you think you'll be eating eggrolls. And sushi. Picking them up with dainty little chopsticks! And everybody will bow to each other all the time. Ha! Listen, Madame Butterfly, GET REAL. Yes, nothing. Nothing here. None of this.

The Gap jeans are too skinny, too fitted. What could you fit in the pockets? You can't even get your hand in the pocket. Okay, yes, the black wool jersey harem pants would work. They're roomy, have an elastic waist and deep pockets, but you see the problem is this: they're *wool* jersey. Wool jersey is like crack to moths. There will be moths . . . and other things. You don't want to know. Smart wool? What the hell does that mean? Like *gifted* wool? *Genius* wool? Okay, tell me this: What's these pants' I.Q.? Yes, I know they're all-season, but believe me, not the seasons we're talking about. You won't want to be wearing black *wool* pants in the heat. Believe me. You'll take one pair of pants, preferably good sturdy cargo pants. CFSW. Fatigues are ideal. Waterproof. Rip-stop. A dark color. Or camouflage. Nothing should be a light color that shows dirt and stains. They don't like to see that. When it's bitter cold, you'll layer the pants over a pair of thick tights. Do you have a good pair of thick tights? Or insulated long underwear? Yes, I suppose silk for long underwear is okay. *Wintersilks?* Hmm. No, I'm not familiar with their catalog or website. Yes, I suppose they would dry quickly. Okay. Put them on. Put those Einstein pants on for now, too, and we'll go to VoA and Goodwill once we're done here—get you outfitted properly—get whatever else you need. Oh, you'll need a tarp, too. No, not a pashmina shawl. A tarp. T.A.R.P. Tarp. You can get them cheap at Family Dollar. $4.99. Right next to VoA. Yes. Blue or green. No. Blue or green only. Vera Bradley? You're kidding. What? You wanna look like The Diaper Bag that Ate Chicago? And pick up a couple of bungee cords, too. You'll see a bin of them just inside the door. All sizes. A buck each.

PAJAMAS

Are you kidding? You will sleep in your clothes.

SWEATERS AND SCARVES

One. Well, if I were you, I'd choose a heavy, serviceable cotton. Cable knit is good. Preferably a cardigan. Or an Army surplus pullover. A hoodie would be better. A hoodie is ideal. Well, okay, the lightweight gray cashmere, but believe me, you'll be sorry. Yes, the silk and angora shawl your niece knitted for you is beautiful, and yes, it would be warm and cozy, but it's too bulky. Impractical. Put it down.

Do you have a scarf, say, a muffler? Something small and warm? Something to protect your neck? What? This? Are you kidding? Messenger of the Gods? *Sheesh.* What were the gods thinking? Probably, like "Here, Herpes—or whatever your name is—get this thing away from me." Collectible, you say? Forget that crap. Isn't that what they said about Beanie Babies? Listen, to tell you the truth, not only is this scarf useless—unless maybe you want to hang yourself—but it's ugly. Personally, I wouldn't be caught dead in it. I don't care if *he* gave it to you. He's dead, right? The dead don't care. Trust me on that. I know. Listen. I don't care if Jesus on a pony gave you that scarf. PUT IT DOWN.

GLOVES

Yes, you'll need gloves. No. No leather. So what if they're lined with rabbit fur? Padded, rubberized gardening gloves are perfect. Or insulated oven mitts. No! Not both!

COATS

No. No. No. No. None of these will do. Fur? Are you for real? No! Not even faux fur. The vintage 100% cashmere Lilli Ann swing coat? What? Are you, like, crazy? Forget about the drape, the cut. You'll need something all-season. Big. Boxy. With a drawstring bottom. Nylon. Ripstop. Lightweight. Sub-zero rated. Waterproof. Dark. With a hood. Army surplus, Goodwill, VoA. I'm sorry. What? More coats? What? Like you had to have *two* of every style black coat on the planet? What is this, like the Noah's Ark of black coats? You know, there's a fine line—a *very* fine line between collecting and hoarding. This, my friend, is HOARDING. Remember what Mahatma Gandhi said: "If you have two coats, give one away." Well, no, I never thought of it that way. How would I know how many loincloths he had? TAKE THAT CAPE OFF!

HATS

A bowler? Are you shittin' me? A velvet beret? The fur-felt fedora? Borsalino? So what? Who cares? Put it down. The top hat? Puh-leese! A mink toque! No! Leopard skin pillbox? Yeah, yeah, iconic, I know the song. Something with earflaps. Here, this one—did you say it's alpaca? from Peru?—this will do just fine. It will fit in your pocket. I know. I know. But the color doesn't really matter. What exactly *is* your color? Autumn? Oh, really? Geez, I would have pegged you for a Summer. Listen. After a week, you'll have no sense of fashion. Or color. It just won't matter. Believe me, you just won't care. All this will go away. Everything will be black and white. CFSW. Simple.

SOCKS

Here, these are perfect. You may take two pairs of these Carhartt insulated moisture-wicking hiking socks. Perfect. I don't care. You pick. Put one pair on. Listen to me. Read my lips: COLOR DOESN'T MATTER. The general rule, though, is: dark. No, never. Never white or cream.

GLASSES

One pair only. I don't care! You pick. Yes, those are cute.

PURSE

No, you will not need a purse. Do you have a backpack? Don't start thinking Gucci or Pucci. Think Goodwill, Family Dollar, VoA. Yes, okay, this little suitcase on wheels. Yes, I see it has a retractable handle. No, I never heard of him. French, eh? Yes, I see all the Vees and fleur-de-lis. Listen. Nobody's going to care if it's really a Hong Kong knock-off. Are you kidding? Nobody will know the difference. Probably the original was a Hong Kong knock-off. And besides, it's really ugly to begin with. But go ahead. Take it. Knock yourself out.

ART

Are you kidding? How would you carry that? No, no art. No heirlooms. No keepsakes. Just forget about that stuff. Geez. What. The. Fuck. Is. That? A fox? Oh, really? Looks like a rat. Where'd ya dig that up? King Tut's tomb? I don't care who it belonged to. Put it down. A disappearing quarter trick? What, you think you're, like, David Copperfield? Why not a box with a head in it like *Señor Wences?* Ha-ha-ha! No, no shadow puppets. Yes, I see how it works. Interesting. I know it's lightweight. Yes, it's very beautiful. Exquisitely tooled. No, I've never been to Bali. Okay, you may take the little brass monkey but only because he will fit in your pocket and because he's good luck, you say. Believe me, you'll need all the luck you can get.

JEWELRY

Are you kidding? No. None. *None whatsoever.* The aurora borealis brooch? It wouldn't last five minutes. Believe me. PEARLS! Ha! You crack me up! No! No Swarovski crystal! No earrings! Take them off. Yes the teapot and teacup earrings are adorable, but WHAT DID I JUST TELL YOU? I don't care if the sardine pin is good luck. You have one good-luck charm. It's the fish or the monkey. You decide. Not both. Yes, you may wear your wedding band. But, let me warn you: don't expect to hold on to it. No, you will not need a watch. You will not want a watch. I don't care if it lights up. Leave it.

COSMETICS

I told you: *No Cosmetics.* Zero. Nada. Zilch. What? Are you deaf? You may take your toothbrush. No, not the electric one! Yes, that's it. Period. Nothing else. No! How many times do I have to say this? Nothing electric. Repeat after me: NOTHING ELECTRIC. Yes, that includes a hair dryer. Believe me. You won't need it. No, no creams or lotions. Your skin will adapt. Yes, I know, but once you forgo these hypoallergenic scrubs and soaps and astringents, you'll get used to it. Your skin will change. Absolutely not. Lip gloss? Mascara? Cream rinse? Never. No. None of this. You will not be coloring your hair or doing your nails. You will not need any of this. No, it will not be necessary. Use your fingers. Perfume? Listen: we're talking Kwell. Ever heard of Kwell? Kwell. K.W.E.L.L. Well, you will. Kwell and Lysol. The neck exerciser? I'm not even going to respond to that. I'm just going to pretend I didn't hear you ask that question. No, you will not need a mirror. Believe me, you will not *want* a mirror. Alright. Keep the damn wig. Just wear it. Put it on. Yeah, yeah, it looks great. Perfect. Nancy Reagan trick-or-treating as Rod Stewart.

PRESCRIPTIONS

You will not need them. You'll run out anyway, so why even take them? Wait. Is that Xanax? What? Did you say back pain? Kidney stones? Oral surgery? Let me see what all you've got there.

ELECTRONICS

Absolutely not. Nothing electronic. Yes, I know it's lightweight. I can see that it's a MacBook Air, but still, you don't need it. I know. I know.

But there will be antibacterial hand sanitizer. Everywhere. You build up your immune system. Besides, you won't care. And you will learn to write differently. Have you ever heard of pen and paper? They will give you these if you ask for them. That's right. You will not need your Blackberry. Who would you call, under the circumstances? Who would want to call you? You'll lose touch with all of them. And you won't care. Throw it away. "Around Me"? Listen, you don't need those apps. Trust me. You won't need a GPS navigator. You'll find your way. There will be guides. Texting? No! And forget the camera. And, no, you will not need your address book. Or your keys. You will not need any of this. All this is superfluous.

MONEY

Credit cards! Forget 'em! They're useless now! Remember? Forget about the rewards and frequent-flier miles. Listen. There are no rewards. And you're not going to be flying anywhere. Get it?

BOOKS

No. No. And NO. You can't take any books. Listen. They're too heavy. Just leave them. I know. I know. It's a signed first edition. Big deal. I know she's your favorite author. Yes, I know the Chekhov thing. The Booger Prize? What's that? Oh, Booker, as in book. Who cares? Listen to me. Ever heard of a library? You don't have to own these things to have access to them. All right, a dictionary. But not that big *American Heritage.* Remember, you're the one who has to carry all this shit. You think you'll have a porter or something? Maybe a donkey or camel? Listen. No. You can't have a shopping cart. You step away from it and BINGO! It's gone. Somebody will take it and everything in it. Trust me on this. You have to hold on to everything at all times.

PENS/STATIONERY

Yes, you may keep your favorite pen. No, not the inlaid pencil box. Okay. Two pens or one pen and one mechanical pencil. These are totally dispensable. Okay, that small Moleskine. But not the big one. Yes, I know they won't be the same, but you will learn to adapt, to appreciate and utilize what's available. And you'll find this kind of stuff everywhere. You just have to look. Always look down when you walk. Don't look up. There's nothing up there. Don't make eye contact with anyone. Rule Number One. Hear me? No one. Eye contact comes later. After you're out there awhile. Your mentor will teach you this art. Then, with a little practice, you'll be able to pinpoint a block away who's a soft-serve, but for now, eyes down. Scan the street, the sidewalk, the gutters, the doorways, the stairwells, the storm drains. Let your eyes sweep over everything. Back and forth. Back and forth. Sweep-sweep-sweep. Like a pendulum. You'll be amazed at what you find. Things will find *you*! No. You will not need your stationery. Leave it.

PHOTOGRAPHS

No. No photo albums. The shoebox—the family photos, the laminated obituaries? Commit them to memory. No way. I know. I know. You may take one wallet-size photo. Well then just fold it to fit in your pocket, for gawd's sake! No. No driver's license, no passport, no I.D. of any kind. You're better off without them. Besides, you'll have a new name.

MUSIC/INSTRUMENTS

No. Yes, I know it's tiny. But believe me, as I said before, you will have no use for electronics. A ukulele? Please. And I suppose you'll want to take your lei and your hula skirt, too, right? And all your favorite Don Ho albums. *Tiny bubbles.* No! The little wooden recorder? Okay, okay, but only because it's lightweight and comes apart.

APPLIANCES/SILVERWARE

No. None of it. Nothing! What did I say? NOTHING ELECTRIC. No small appliances. No! No blender. A blender would fall into the category of small appliance. Yes, I can see it's a Cuisinart. I told you: I can see. I can read. You think I'm blind? You think I'm, like, Stevie Wonder? Blind Lemon Jefferson? Listen. The blender is *useless*. Shut up. No energy drinks. No smoothies. No frozen margaritas. Ever hear of Night Train?

MD 20/20? Thunderbird? Everclear? High Gravity? Well, believe me, you will. Yeah, right. Top shelf. Top shelf in a dog house.

No, no silverware either. You're being ridiculous. Yes, I can see the monogram. I'm not blind. I know the alphabet. I see the big fuckin' *W* on your spoon. Listen to me. Stop crying. Put it down. Give it to me! Stop! Listen. You will be eating out. You don't need your own silverware. Listen. STOP IT! You've got to be tough. It's tough out there. You're not the only one who's ended up like this. Lots of other people have had monogrammed silverware and other shit you wouldn't believe. I mean, you have no idea what others have relinquished. Okay. Okay, the little antique pocketknife with the mother-of-pearl handle—the one your father gave you on your twelfth birthday—that may come in handy. Take that. And here, take this headlamp hanging by the back door. And, here: this role of duct tape. Now give me the spoon. Drop it!

THE DOG

And just how will you take care of a dog? I know. I know. Yes, I believe you, I understand, but listen to me: the dog will be a burden. It would be best if you separated yourself from the dog right now. And, trust me, the dog will not be happy where you're going. It's like children. Where you're going is no place for those who can't fend for themselves. That's ridiculous. A Chihuahua? Protection? But, okay. Stop crying. Listen. Stop crying. If you insist. A friendly little dog might be an asset.

Ouch! You fuckin' little bastard! Yes, I can see he's not too friendly. You could have told me, though, before I tried to pet him. *I did not provoke him!* Well, he better get used to strangers. Everyone's a stranger out there. I think you'll regret this decision, but, yes, okay, take the damn little rat. See if I care. Sure, take his damn leash, too. Take the stupid little ball. The hedgehog is too big. It's bigger than him. Leave it. His bed? It's extra weight, but yes, okay, yes, you could roll it up, like you say, and strap it on your ugly suitcase with a bungee cord. And, well, if he predeceases you, why then I guess you could use his little bed as a pillow. It doesn't hurt to have a pillow. But let me tell you: it won't last. Nothing lasts. No, no heartworm pills. He will be living like you, taking chances. It's all about chance. Chance. Fate. Serendipity. Weather. CFSW.

OTHER

The hula hoop? That was a joke, right? You know, you're kind of funny. In your own way. That's good. Good. Keep it up.

Ready? Come on, Madame Butterfly. Chop-chop. You, too, Topo Gigio or Toto or whatever your name is. There'll be plenty to sniff where you're going. Listen. Don't bother to lock it! Just leave it! Leave the key! No you don't have to take one last look. So what if you left the stove on? On second thought, go ahead. Run back in and turn the stove ON. Turn all the burners on HIGH. Turn the oven to BROIL. Listen. I was just kidding. Stop sniffling. Come on. Buck up! Get a grip. It doesn't matter if you forgot anything. Come, now. Come on! You, too, Pancho Villa. Get the lead outta your pants. I know it's hard. Come on! Don't look back. Never turn around. Always look ahead. Just keep walking. Remember, head down, eyes like a pendulum. Back and forth and back and forth. Come on, now! Get a grip. Take my hand. *Lions, and tigers, and bears, Oh my! Lions, and tigers, and bears, Oh my!* That's it. *Simba, Timba! Timba, unGawa!* That's it. Back and forth and . . . you know . . . I hate to mention this, but the wheels on that thing are never gonna last. Look: one of them's gone all cattywampus already.

Author's Acknowledgments

Thank you to Etruscan Press; Bonnie Culver and the faculty and students of the Wilkes University Low-Residency Creative Writing Program; the West Virginia Wesleyan College Low-Residency Creative Writing Program; and the Thornton Writer-in-Residence Program at Lynchburg College. In particular, thank you to Laura Long, Cristina Negrón, Starr Troup, Tara Caimi, James Cihlar, Julianne Popovec, Carey Black, Cameron Lohr, Eva Gauthier, Erin Miele, Dawn Zera, Jaclyn Fowler, Jenny Bent, and Caroline Jennings. And with special thanks to Phil Brady, Bob Mooney, and Beverly Donofrio. And, always, K.O.

Books from Etruscan Press

Venison | Thorpe Moeckel
So Late, So Soon | Carol Moldaw
The Widening | Carol Moldaw
White Vespa | Kevin Oderman
The Shyster's Daughter | Paula Priamos
Saint Joe's Passion | JD Schraffenberger
Lies Will Take You Somewhere | Sheila Schwartz
Fast Animal | Tim Seibles
American Fugue | Alexis Stamatis
The Casanova Chronicles | Myrna Stone
The White Horse: A Colombian Journey | Diane Thiel
The Fugitive Self | John Wheatcroft

Etruscan Press Is Proud of Support Received From

Wilkes University

Youngstown State University

The Raymond John Wean Foundation

The Ohio Arts Council

The Stephen & Jeryl Oristaglio Foundation

The Nathalie & James Andrews Foundation

The National Endowment for the Arts

The Ruth H. Beecher Foundation

The Bates-Manzano Fund

The New Mexico Community Foundation

The Gratia Murphy Endowment

Founded in 2001 with a generous grant from the Oristaglio Foundation, Etruscan Press is a nonprofit cooperative of poets and writers working to produce and promote books that nurture the dialogue among genres, achieve a distinctive voice, and reshape the literary and cultural histories of which we are a part.

etruscan press
www.etruscanpress.org

Etruscan Press books may be ordered from

Consortium Book Sales and Distribution
800.283.3572
www.cbsd.com

Small Press Distribution
800.869.7553
www.spdbooks.org

Etruscan Press is a 501(c)(3) nonprofit organization.
Contributions to Etruscan Press are tax deductible
as allowed under applicable law.
For more information, a prospectus,
or to order one of our titles,
contact us at books@etruscanpress.org.